Harold MacGrath

The Voice in the Fog

Harold MacGrath

The Voice in the Fog

ISBN/EAN: 9783955630775

Auflage: 1

Erscheinungsjahr: 2013

Erscheinungsort: Bremen, Deutschland

@ Leseklassiker in Access Verlag GmbH, Fahrenheitstr. 1, 28359
Bremen. Alle Rechte beim Verlag und bei den jeweiligen
Lizenzgebern.

Table of Contents

Kitty Killigrew

CHAPTER I

Fog.

A London fog, solid, substantial, yellow as an old dog's tooth or a jaundiced eye. You could not look through it, nor yet gaze up and down it, nor over it; and you only thought you saw it. The eye became impotent, untrustworthy; all senses lay fallow except that of touch; the skin alone conveyed to you with promptness and no incertitude that this thing had substance. You could feel it; you could open and shut your hands and sense it on your palms, and it penetrated your clothes and beaded your spectacles and rings and bracelets and shoe-buckles. It was nightmare, bereft of its pillows, grown somnambulistic; and London became the antechamber to Hades, lackeyed by idle dreams and peopled by mistakes.

There is something about this species of fog unlike any other in the world. It sticks. You will find certain English cousins of yours, as far away from London as Hong-Kong, who are still wrapt up snugly in it. Happy he afflicted with strabismus, for only he can see his nose before his face. In the daytime you become a fish, to wriggle over the ocean's floor amid strange flora and fauna, such as ash-cans and lamp-posts and venders' carts and cab-horses and sandwich-men. But at night you are neither fish, bird nor beast.

The night was May thirteenth; never mind the year; the date should suffice: and a Walpurgis night, if you please, without any Mendelssohn to interpret it.

That happy line of Milton's — "Pandemonium, the high capital of Satan and his peers" — fell upon London like Elijah's mantle. Confusion and his cohort of synonyms (why not?) raged up and down thoroughfare and side-street and alley, east and west, danced before palace and tenement alike: all to the vast amusement of the gods, to the mild annoyance of the half-gods (in Mayfair), and to the complete rout of all mortals a-foot or a-cab. Imagine: militant suffragettes trying to set fire to the prime minister's mansion, *Siegfried* being sung at the opera, and a yellow London fog!

The press about Covent Garden was a mathematical problem over which Euclid would have shed bitter tears and hastily retired to his arbors and citron tables. Thirty years previous (to the thirteenth of May, not Euclid) some benighted beggar invented the Chinese puzzle; and tonight, many a frantic policeman would have preferred it, sitting with the scullery maid and the pantry near by. Simple matter to shift about little blocks of wood with the tip of one's finger; but cabs and carriages and automobiles, each driver anxious to get out ahead of his neighbor! — not to mention the shouting and the din and discord of horns and whistles and sirens and rumbling engines!

"It's hard luck," said Crawford, sympathetically. "It will be half an hour before they get this tangle straightened out."

"I shouldn't mind, Jim, if it weren't for Kitty," replied his wife. "I am worried about her."

2

"Well, I simply could not drag her into this coupé and get into hers myself. She's a heady little lady, if you want to know. As it is, she'll get back to the hotel quicker than we shall. Her cab is five up. If you wish, I'll take a look in and see if she's all right."

"Please do;" and she smiled at him, lovely, enchanting.

"You're the most beautiful woman in all this world!"

"Am I?"

Click! The light went out. There was a smothered laugh; and when the light flared up again, the aigrette in her copper-beech hair was all askew.

"If anybody saw us!" — secretly pleased and delighted, as any woman would have been who possessed a husband who was her lover all his waking hours.

"What! in this fog? And a lot I'd care if they did. Now, don't stir till I come back; and above all, keep the light on."

"And hurry right back; I'm getting lonesome already."

He stepped out of the coupé. Harlequin, and Colombine, and Humpty-Dumpty; shapes which came out of nowhere and instantly vanished into nothing, for all the world like the absurd pantomimes of his boyhood days. He kept close to the curb, scrutinizing the numbers as he went along. Never had he seen such a fog. Two paces away from the curb a headlight became an effulgence. Indeed, there were a thousand lights jammed in the street, and the fog above absorbed the radiance, giving the scene a touch of Brocken. All that was needed was a witch on a broomstick. He counted five vehicles, and stopped. The door-window was down.

"Miss Killigrew?" he said.

"Yes. Is anything wrong?"

"No. Just wanted to see if you were all right. Better let me take your place and you ride with Mrs. Crawford."

"Good of you; but you've had enough trouble. I shall stay right here."

"Where's your light?"

"The globe is broken. I'd rather be in the dark. Its fun to look about. I never saw anything to equal it."

"Not very cheerful. We'll be held up at least half an hour. You are not afraid?"

"What, I?" She laughed. "Why should I be afraid? The wait will not matter. But the truth is, I'm worried about mother. She would go to that suffragette meeting; and I understand they have tried to burn up the prime minister's house."

"Fine chance! But don't you worry. Your mother's a sensible woman. She'll get back to the hotel, if she isn't there already."

"I wish she had not gone. Father will be tearing his hair and twigging the whole Savoy force by the ears."

Crawford smiled. Readily enough he could conjure up the picture of Mr. Killigrew, short, thick-set, energetic, raging back and forth in the lobby, offering to buy taxicabs outright, the hotel, and finally the city of London itself; typically money-mad American that he was. Crawford wanted to laugh, but he compromised by saying: "He must be very careful of that hair of his; he hasn't much left."

"And he pulls out a good deal of it on my account. Poor dad! Why in the world should I marry a title?"

"Why, indeed!"

"Mrs. Crawford was beautiful tonight. There wasn't a beauty at the opera to compare with her. Royalties are frumps, aren't they? And that ruby! I don't see how she dares wear it!"

"I am not particularly fond of it; but it's a fad of hers. She likes to wear it on state occasions. I have often wondered if it is really the Nana Sahib's ruby, as her uncle claimed. Driver, the Savoy, and remember it carefully; the Savoy."

"Yes, sir; I understand, sir. But we'll all be some time, sir. Collision forward is what holds us, sir."

Alone again, Kitty Killigrew leaned back, thinking of the man who had just left her and of his beautiful wife. If only she might some day have a romance like theirs! Presently she peered out of the off-window. A brood of *Siegfried*-dragons prowled about, now going forward a little, now swerving, now pausing; lurid eyes and threatening growls.

Once upon a time, in her pigtail days, when her father was going to be rich and was only half-way between the beginning and the end of his ambition, Kitty had gone to a tent-circus. Among other things she had looked wonderingly into the dim, blurry glass-tank of the "human fish," who was at that moment busy selling photographs of himself. To-night, in searching for comparisons, this old forgotten picture recurred to her mind; blithely memory brought it forth and threw it upon the screen. All London had become a glass-tank, filled with human pollywogs.

She did not want to marry a title; she did not want to marry money; she did not want to marry at all. Poor kindly dad, who believed that she could be made happy only by marrying a title. As if she was not as happy now as she was ever destined to be!

Voices. Two men were speaking near the curb-door. She turned her head involuntarily in this direction. There were no lights in the frontage before which stood her cab, which intervened between the Brocken haze in the street, throwing a square of Stygian shadow against the fog, with right and left angles of aureola. She could distinguish no shapes.

"Cheer up, old top; you're in hard luck."

"I'm a bally ass."

"No, no; only a ripping good sporty game all the way through."

Oddly enough, Kitty sensed the irony. She wondered if the speaker's companion did.

"Well, a wager's a wager."

"And you're the last chap to welch a square bet. What's the odds? My word, I didn't urge you to change the stakes."

"Didn't you?"

The voice was young and pleasant; and Kitty was sure that the owner's face was even as pleasant as his voice. What had he wagered and lost?

"If you're really hard pressed…"

"Hard pressed! Man, I've nothing in God's world but two guineas, six."

"Oh, I say now!"

"Its the truth."

"If a fiver will help you…"

"Thanks. A wager's a wager. I've lost. I was a bally fool to play cards. Deserve what I got. Six months; that's the agreement. A madman's wager; but I'll stick."

"Six months; twelve o'clock, midnight, November thirteenth. It's the date, old boy; that's what hoodooed you, as the Americans say."

Kitty wasn't sure that the speaker was English; if he was, he had lost the insular significance of his vowels. Still, it was, in its way, as pleasant a voice as the other's. There was no doubt about the younger man; he was English to the core, English in his love of chance, English in his loyalty to his word; stupidly English. That he was the younger was a trifling matter to deduce: no young man ever led his elder into mischief, harmful or innocuous.

"Six months. It's a joke, my boy; a great big laugh for you and me, when there's nothing left in life but toddies and churchwardens. Six months."

"I dare say I can hang on till that time is over. Well, good night! No letters, no addresses."

"Exact terms. Six months from date I'll be cooling my heels in your ante-room."

"Cavenaugh, if it's anything else except a joke..."

"Oh, rot! It was your suggestion. I tell you, it's a lark, nothing more. A gentleman's word."

"I'll start for my diggings."

"Ride home with me; my cab's here somewhere."

"No, thanks. I've got a little thinking to do and prefer to be alone. Good night."

"And good luck go with you. Deuce take it, if you feel so badly..."

There was no reply; and Kitty decided that the younger man had gone on. Silence; or rather, she no longer heard the speakers. Then a low chuckle came to her and this chuckle broadened into ironic laughter; and she knew that Mephisto was abroad. What had been the wager; and what was the meaning of the six months? It is instinctive in woman to interpret the human voice correctly, especially when the eyes are not distracted by physical presentations. This man outside, whoever and whatever he was, deep in her heart Kitty knew that he was not going to play fair. What a disappointing world it was! — to set these human voices ringing in her ears, and then to take them out of her life forever!

Still the din of horns and whistles and sirens, still the shouting. Would they never move on? She was hungry. She wanted to get back to the hotel, to learn what had happened to her mother. Militant suffragettes, indeed! A pack of mad witches, who left their brooms behind kitchen doors when they ought to be wielding them about dusty corners. Woman never won anything by using brickbats and torches: which proved on the face of it that these militants were inefficient, irresponsible, and un-learned in history. Poor simpletons! Had not theirs always been the power behind the throne? What more did they want?

Her cogitations were peculiarly interrupted. The door opened, and a man plumped down beside her.

"Enid, it looks as if we'd never get out of this hole. Have you got your collar up?"

Numb and terrified, Kitty felt the man's hands fumbling about her neck.

"Where's your sable stole? You women beat the very devil for thoughtlessness. A quid to a farthing, you've left it in the box, and I'll have to go back for it, providing they'll let me in. And it's midnight, if a minute."

Pressing herself tightly into her corner, Kitty managed to gasp: "My name is not Enid, sir. You have mistaken your carriage."

"What? Good heavens!" Almost instantly a match sparkled and flared. His eyes, screened behind his hand, palm outward (a perfectly natural action, yet nicely calculated), beheld a pretty, charming face, large Irish blue eyes (a bit startled at this moment), and a head of hair as shiny-black as polished Chinese blackwood. The match, still burning, curved like a falling star through the window. "A thousand pardons, madam! Very stupid of me. Quite evident that I am lost. I beg your pardon again, and hope I have not annoyed you."

He was gone before she could form any retort. Where had she heard that voice before? With a little shudder — due to the thought of those cold strange fingers feeling about her throat — her hands went up. Instantly she cried aloud in dismay. Her sapphires! They had vanished!

CHAPTER II

Daniel Killigrew, of Killigrew and Company (sugar, coffee and spices), was in a towering rage; at least, he towered one inch above his normal height, which was five feet six. Like an animal recently taken in captivity he trotted back and forth through the corridors, in and out of the office, to and from the several entrances, blowing the while like a grampus. All he could get out of these infernally stupid beings was "Really, sir!" He couldn't get a cab, he couldn't get a motor, he couldn't get anything. Manager, head-clerk, porter, doorman and page, he told them, one and all, what a dotty old spoof of a country they lived in; that they were all dead-alive persons, fit to be neither under nor above earth; that they wouldn't be one-two in a race with January molasses — "Treacle, I believe you call it here!" And what did they say to this scathing arraignment? Yes, what did they say? "Really, sir!" He knew and hoped it would happen: if ever Germany started war, it would be over before these Britishers made up their minds that there was a war. A hundred years ago they had beaten Napoleon (with the assistance of Spain, Austria, Germany and Russia), and were now resting.

Quarter to one, and neither wife nor daughter; outside there, somewhere in the fog; and he could not go to them. It was maddening. Molly might be arrested and Kitty lost. Served him right; he should have put his foot down. The idea of Molly being allowed to go with those rattle-pated women! Suffragettes! A "Bah!" exploded with a loud report. Hereafter he would show who voted in the Killigrew family. Poor man! He was made of that unhappy mental timber which agrees thoughtlessly to a proposition for the sake of peace and then regrets it in the name of war. His wife and daughter twisted him round their little fingers and then hunted cover when he found out what they had done.

He went out again to the main entrance and smoked himself headachy. He hated London. He had always hated it in theory, now he hated it in fact. He hated tea, buttered muffins, marmalade, jam, toast, cricket, box hedges three hundred years old, ruins, and the checkless baggage system, the wet blankets called newspapers. All the racial hatred of his forebears (Tipperary born) surged hot and wrathful in his veins. At the drop of a hat he would have gone to war, individually, with all England. "Really, sir!" Nothing but that, when he was dying of anxiety!

A taxicab drew up before the canopy. He knew it was a taxicab because he could hear the sound of the panting engine. The curb-end of the canopy was curtained by the abominable fog. Mistily a forlorn figure emerged. The doorman started leisurely toward this figure. Killigrew pushed him aside violently. Molly, with her hat gone, her hair awry, her dress torn, her gloves ragged, her eyes puffed! He sprang toward her, filled with Berserker rage. Who had dared.

"Give the man five pounds," she whispered. "I promised it."

"Five..."

"Give it to him! Good heavens, do I look as if I

were joking? Pay him, pay him!"

Killigrew counted out five sovereigns, perhaps six, he was not sure. The chauffeur swooped them up, and set off.

"Molly Killigrew..."

"Not a word till I get to the rooms. Hurry! Daniel, if you say anything I shall fall down!"

He led her to the lift. Curious glances followed, but these signified nothing. On a night such as this was there would be any number of accidents. Once in the living-room of the luxurious suite, Mrs. Killigrew staggered over to the divan and tumbled down upon it. She began to cry hysterically.

"Molly, old girl! Molly!" He put his arm tenderly across her heaving shoulders and kneeled. His old girl! Love crowded out all other thoughts. Money-mad he might be, but he never forgot that Molly had once fried his meat and peeled his potatoes and darned his socks. "Molly, what has happened? Who did this? Tell me, and I'll kill him!"

"Dan, when they started up the street for the prime minister's house, I could not get out of the crowd. I was afraid to. It was so foggy you had to follow the torches. I did not know what they were about till the police rushed us. One grabbed me, but I got away." All this between sobs. "Dan, I don't want to be a suffragette." Sob. "I don't want to vote." Sob.

And for the first time that night Killigrew smiled.

"Where's Kitty?"

He started to his feet. "She hasn't got back from the opera yet. She'll be the death of me, one of these fine days. You know her. Like as not she's stepped out of her cab to see what's going on, and has lost herself."

"But the Crawfords were with her."

"Would that make any difference with Kitty if she wanted to get out? I told her not to wear any jewels, but she wouldn't mind me. She never does. I haven't any authority except in my offices. You and Kitty…"

"Don't scold!"

"All right; I won't. But, all the same, you and the girl need checking."

"Daniel, it was only because I wanted something to occupy myself with. It's no fun for me to sit still in my house and watch everybody else work. The butler orders the meals, the housekeeper takes charge of the linen, the footman the carriages. Why, I can't find a button to sew on anything any more. I only wanted something to do."

Killigrew did not smile this time. Here was the whole matter in a nutshell: she wanted something to do. And there were thousands of others just like her. Man-like, he forgot that women needed something more than money and attention from an army of servants. He had his offices, his stock-ticker, his warfare. Not because she wanted to vote, but because she wanted and needed something to do.

"Molly, old girl, I begin to see. I'm going to finance a home-bureau of charity. I mean it. Fifty thousand the year to do with as you like. No hospitals, churches, heathen; but the needy and deserving near by. You can send boys to college and girls to schools; and Kitty'll be glad to be your lieutenant. I never had a college education. Not that I ever needed it," — with sudden truculence in his tone. "But it might be a good thing for some of the rising generations in my tenements. I'll leave the choice to you. And when it comes to voting, why, tell me which way to vote, and I'll do it. I'll be a bull moose, if you say so."

"You're the kindest man in the world, Dan, and I'm an old fool of a woman!"

Kitty burst into the room, star-eyed, pale. "Mother!" She sped to her mother's side. "Oh, I felt it in my bones that something was going to happen!"

"Think of it, Kitty dear; your mother, fighting with a policeman! Oh, it was frightful!"

"Never mind, mumsy," Kitty soothed. She rang for the maid, a thing her father had not thought to do. And when her mother was snug in bed, her head in cooling bandages, her face and hands bathed in refreshing cologne, Kitty returned to her father, "Dad, you mustn't say a word to mother about it, but I've been robbed."

"What?"

"My necklace. And I could not identify the thief if he stood before me this very minute. The interior light was out of order. He entered, pretending he had made a mistake. He called me Enid and told me to put up my collar; touched my neck with his hands. I was so astonished that I could not move. Finally I managed to explain that he had made a mistake. He apologized and got out; and it is quite evident that the necklace went with him."

"Can't you remember the least thing about him?"

"Nothing, absolutely nothing."

"Where were the Crawfords?"

"I did not wait to see them. My cab was ahead of theirs. What shall we do?"

"Notify the police; it's all we can do. They cost me an even ten thousand, Kitty. And I told you not to wear them on a night like this. I'm discouraged. I want to get out of this blasted country. I'm hoo-dooed." Killigrew walked the floor. He took out a cigar, eyed it thoughtfully, and returned it to his pocket. "Because they happen to be born in this smoke, they think the way they do things is the last word on the subject. I'd like to show them."

"Dad," — with a bit of a smile, — "I know what the trouble is. You want to go home."

"And that's the truth. This is the first trip abroad I ever took with you and your mother, and it's going to be the last. I can't live out of my element, which is hurry and bustle and getting things done quickly. I'm a fish out of water. I want to go home; I want to see the Giants wallop the Cubs; and I want my two-weeks' bass fishing. But I'll hang on till the end of June as I promised. Ten thousand in sapphires you couldn't match in a hundred years, and Molly coming in banged up like a prize-fighter! ... Someone at the door."

It proved to be Crawford.

"Glad you got back safely," he said relievedly.

"Had her necklace stolen," replied Killigrew briefly.

"You don't mean to say..."

Kitty recounted her amazing adventure.

"And my wife's ruby is gone." Crawford made the disclosure simply. He was a quiet man; he had learned the futility of gestures, of wasting words in lamentation.

"Good gracious!" exclaimed Kitty.

"The windows of the cab were down. I stood outside, smoking to pass the time. Suddenly I heard Mrs. Crawford cry out. A hand had reached in from the off side, clutched the pendant, twisted it off, and was gone. All quicker than I can tell it. I tried to give chase, but it was utter folly. I couldn't see anything two feet away. Mrs. Crawford is a bit knocked up over it. Rather sinister stone, if its history is a true one: the Nana Sahib's ruby, you know. For the jewel itself I don't care. I never liked to see her wear it."

Killigrew threw up his hands. "And this is the London you've been bragging about to me! How much was the ruby worth?"

"Don't know; nobody does. It's one of those jewels you can't set a price on. He will not be able to dispose of it in its present shape. He'll break it up and sell the pieces, and that's the shame of it. Think of the infernal cleverness of the man! Two or three hundred vehicles stalled in the street, fog so thick you couldn't see your hand before your face. Simple game for a man with ready wit. And the police busy at the two ends of the block, trying to straighten out the tangle. Mrs. Crawford says that the hand was white, slender and well kept. It came in swiftly and accurately. The man had been watching and waiting. She was so unprepared for the act that she didn't even try to catch the hand. I have notified Scotland Yard. But you can't hunt down a hand. I'm willing to wager that we'll neither of us ever see the gems again."

"He must have come directly from your carriage to mine," said Kitty. "I am heart-broken."

"One of the tricks of fate. Glad you got back all right. We were mightily worried. Come over across the hall at nine to-morrow, all of you, for breakfast. Don't fuss up. And we'll talk over the affair and plan what's to be done. Good night."

"I like that young man," declared Killigrew emphatically. "He's the real article. American to the backbone; a millionaire who doesn't splurge. Well," sighing regretfully, "he was born to it, and I had to dig for mine. But I can't get it through my head why he wants to excavate mummies when he could dig up potatoes with some profit."

"Dad, find me an earl or a duke like Mr. Crawford, and I'll marry him just as fast as you like."

"Kittibudget, I'm not so strong for dukes as I was. Your mother will have a black eye in the morning, or I don't know a shindy when I see it. Now, hike off to bed. I'm all in."

"You poor old dad! I worry you to death."

She threw her lovely arms about his neck and kissed him.

"Well, you're worth it. Kitty, I've had a jolt to-night. You marry whom you blame please. I've been doing some tall thinking. Make your own romance, duke or dry-goods clerk. You'd never hook up with anything that wasn't a man. You're Irish. If he happens to be made, all well and good; if not, why, I'll undertake to make him. And that's a bargain. I don't want any alimony money in the Killigrew family."

She kissed him again and went into her bedroom. Kind-hearted, impulsive old dad! In a week's time he would forget all about this heart-to-heart talk, and shoo away every male who hadn't a title or a million, or who wasn't due to fall heir to one or the other. Nevertheless, she had long since made up her mind to build her own romance. That was her right, and she did not propose to surrender it to anybody. Her weary head on the pillow, she thought of the voices in the fog. "A wager's a wager."

The next morning the fog was not quite so thick; that is, in places there were holes and punctures. You saw a man's face and torso, but neither hat nor legs. Again, you saw the top of a cab bowling along, but no horse: phantasmally.

Breakfast in Crawford's suite was merry

enough. Misfortune was turned into jest. At least, they made a fine show of it; which is characteristic of people who bow to the inevitable whenever confronted by it. Crawford was passing his cigars, when a page was announced. The boy entered briskly, carrying a tray upon which reposed a small package.

"By special messenger, sir. It was thought you might be liking to have it at once, sir." The page pocketed the shilling politely and departed.

"That's the first bit of live work I've seen anybody do in this hotel," commented Killigrew, striking a match.

"I have stopped here often," said Crawford, "and they are familiar with my wishes. Excuse me till I see what this is."

The quartet at the table began chatting again, about the fog, what they intended doing in Paris, sunshiny Paris. By and by Crawford came over quietly and laid something on the table before his wife's plate.

It was the Nana Sahib's ruby, so-called.

CHAPTER III

That same morning, at eleven precisely (when an insolent west wind sprang up and tore the fog into ribbons and scarves and finally blew it into smithereens, channelward) there stood before the windows of a famous haberdashery in the Strand a young man, twenty-four years of age, typically English, beardless, hair clipped neatly about his neck and temples, his skin fresh colored, his body carefully but thriftily clothed. Smooth-skinned he was about the eyes and nose and mouth, unmarked by dissipation; and he stood straight; and by the set of his shoulders (not particularly deep or wide) you would infer that when he looked at you he would look straight. Pity, isn't it, that you never really can tell what a man is inside by drawing up your brief from what he is outside. There is always the heel of Achilles somewhere; trust the devil to find that.

Of course you wish to know forthwith who returned the ruby, and why. As our statesmen say, regarding any important measure for public welfare, the time is not yet ripe. Besides, the young man I am describing had never heard of the Nana Sahib's ruby, unless vaguely in some Sepoy Mutiny tale.

His expression at this moment was rather mournful. He was regretting the thirty shillings the week he had for several years drawn regularly in this shop. Inside there he had introduced the Raglan shirt, the Duke of Westminster four-in-hand, and the Churchill batwing collar. He longed to enter and plead for reinstatement, but his new-found pride refused to budge his legs door-ward. Thirty shillings, twelve for his "third floor back," and the rest for clothes and books and simple amusements. What a whirl he had been in, this past fortnight!

He pulled at his chin, shook his head and turned away. No, he simply could not do it. What! suffer himself to be laughed at behind his back? Impossible, a thousand times no! At the first news stand he bought two or three morning papers, and continued on to his lodgings. He must leave England at once, but the question was — How?

It was a comfortable room, as "third floor backs" go. He read the "want" advertisements carefully, and at length paused at a paragraph which seemed to suit his fancy perfectly. "Cabin stewards wanted — White Star Line — New York and Liverpool." He cut out the clipping, folded it and stored it away. Then he proceeded to pack up his belongings, not a very laborious affair.

Manuscripts. He riffled the pages ruefully. Sonnets and chant-royals and epics, fine and lofty in spirit; so fine indeed that they easily sifted through every editorial office in London. There was even a bulky romance. He had read so much about the enormous royalties which American authors received for their work, and English authors who were popular on the other side, that his ambition had been frenetically stirred. The fortunes such men as Maundering and Piffle and Drool made! And all he had accomplished so far had been the earnest support of the postal service. Far back at the beginning he had been unfortunate enough to sell a sonnet for ten shillings. Alack! You sell your first sonnet, you win your first hand at cards, and then the passion has you.

Poetry was a drug on the market. Nobody read it (or wrote it) these days; and any one who attempted to sell it was clearly mad. Oh, a jingle for Punch might pass, you know; something clever, with a snapper to it. But epic poetry? Sonnets? Why, didn't you know that there wasn't a magazine going that did not have some sub-editor who could whack out fourteen lines in fourteen minutes, whenever a page needed filling up? These things he had been told times without number. And Maundering, Piffle and Drool had long since cornered the romance market. The King's Highway had become No Thoroughfare.

America. He would go to the land of the brave (when occasion demanded) and the free (if you were imaginative). Having packed his trunk and valise, he departed for Liverpool. Besides, America was all that was left; he was at the end of his rope.

What a rollicking old fraud life was! Swung out of his peaceful orbit, by the legerdemain of death; no longer a humble steady star but a meteor; bumping as yet darkly against the planets; and then this monumental folly which had returned him to the old orbit but still in meteoric form, without peace or means of livelihood! An ass, indeed, if ever there was one.

He eventually arrived at his destination, lied blithely to the chief steward, and was assigned to the first-class cabins on the promenade deck, simply because his manner was engaging and his face pleasing to the eye. The sea? He had never been on it but once, and then only in a rowboat. A good sailor? Perhaps. Chicken and barley broths at eleven; the captain's table in the dining-saloon, breakfast, luncheon and dinner; cabin housekeeper and luggage man at the ports; and always a natty, stiffly starched jacket with a metal number; and "Yes, sir!" and "No, sir!" and "Thank you, sir!" his official vocabulary. Fine job for a poet!

It was all in the game he was going to play with fate. A chap who could sell flamingo ties to gentlemen with purple noses, and shirts with attached cuffs to coal-porters ought not to worry over such a simple employment as cabin-steward on board an ocean liner.

Early the next morning they left port, with only a few first-class passengers. The heavy travel was coming from the west, not going that way. The series of cabins under his stewardship were vacant. Therefore, with the thoroughness of his breed, he set about to learn "ship"; and by the time the first bugle for dinner blew, he knew port from starboard, boat-deck from main, and many other things, some unknown to the chief-steward who had made a hundred and twenty voyages on this very ship.

Beautiful weather; a mild southwest blow, with a moderate beam-sea; only the deck *would* come up smack against the soles of his boots in a most unexpected and aggravating manner. But after the third day out, he found his sea-legs and learned how to "lean." From two till five his time was his own, and a very good deal of this time he devoted to Henley and Morris and Walt Whitman, an ancient brier between his teeth and a canister of excellent tobacco at his elbow. Odd, isn't it, that an Englishman without his pipe is as incomplete as a Manx cat, which, as doubtless you know, has no tail. After all, does a Manx cat know that it is incomplete? Let me say, then, as incomplete as a small boy without pockets.

Toward his fellow stewards he was friendly without being companionable; and as they were of a decent sort, they let him go his way.

Several times during the voyage he opened his trunk and took out the manuscripts. Hang it, they weren't so bally bad. If he could still re-read them, after an hour or two with Henley, there must be some merit to them.

One afternoon he sat alone on the edge of his bunk. The sun was pouring into the porthole; intermittently it flashed over him. Suddenly and alertly he got up, looked out, listened intently, then stepped back into the cabin and locked the door. Again he listened. There was no sound except the steady heart-beats of the great engines below. He sat down sidewise, took out the chamois bag which hung around his neck, and poured the contents out on the blanket. Blue stones, rather dull at first; but ah! when the sun awoke the fires in them: blue as the flower o' the corn, the flame of burning sulphur. He gathered them up and slowly trickled them through his fingers. Sapphires, unset, beautiful as a woman's eyes. He replaced them in the chamois bag; and for the rest of the afternoon went about his affairs preoccupiedly, grave as a bishop under his miter. For, all said and done, he had much to be grave about.

In one of the panels of the partition which separated the cabin from the next, there was a crack. A human eye could see through it very well. And did.

My young poet had "signed on" under the name of Thomas Webb. It was not assumed. For years he had been known in the haberdashery as Webb. There was more to it, however; there was a tail to the kite. The English have an inordinate fondness for hyphens, for mother's family name and grandmother's family name and great-grandmother's, with the immediate paternal cognomen as a period. Thomas' full name was a rosary, if you like, of yeomen, of soldiers, of farmers, of artists, of gentle bloods, of dreamers. The latest transfusion of blood is always most powerful in effect upon the receiver; and as Thomas' father had died in penury for the sake of an idea, it was in order that the son should be something of a dreamer too. Poetry is but an expression of life seen through dreams.

His father had been a scholar, risen from the people; his mother had been gentle. From his seventh year the boy had faced life alone. He had never gone with the stream but had always found lodgment in the backwaters. There is no employment quieter, peacefuller than that of a clerk in a haberdashery. From Mondays till Saturdays, calm; a perfect environment for a poet. You would be surprised to learn of the vast army of poets and novelists and dramatists who dispense four-in-hands, collars, buttons and hosiery six days in the week and who go a-picnicking on the seventh, provided it does not rain.

Thomas had an idea. It was not a reflection of

his lamented father's; it was wholly his own. He wanted to be loved. His father's idea had been to love; thus, humanity had laughed him into the grave. So it will be seen that Thomas' idea was the more sensible of the two.

The voyage was uneventful. Blue day followed blue day. When at length the great port of New York loomed in the distance, Thomas felt a thrilling in his spine. Perhaps yonder he might make his fortune; no matter what else he did, that remained to be accomplished, for he was a fortune-hunter, of the ancient type; that is, he expected to work for it. Shore leave would be his, and if during that time he found nothing, why, he was determined to finish the summer as a steward; and by fall he would have enough in wages and tips to give him a start in life. At present he could jingle but seven-and-six in his pocket; and jingle it frequently he did, to assure himself that it was not wearing away.

An important tug came bustling alongside. By the yellow flag he knew that it carried the quarantine officials, inspectors, and a few privileged citizens. Among others who came aboard Thomas noted a sturdy thick-chested man in a derby hat — bowler, Thomas called it. Quietly this man sought the captain and handed him what looked to Thomas like a cablegram. The captain read it and shook his head. Thomas overheard a little of their conversation.

"You're welcome to look about, Mr. Haggerty; but I don't think you'll find the person you seek."

"If you don't mind, I'll take a prowl. Special case, Captain. Mr. Killigrew thought perhaps I'd see a face I knew."

"Valuable?"

"Fine sapphires. A chance that they may come int' this port. They haven't yet."

"Your customs inspectors ought to be able to help you," observed the captain, hiding a smile. "Nothing but motes can slip through their fingers."

"Sometimes they're tripped up," replied Haggerty. "A case like this is due t' slip through. I'll take a look."

Thomas heard no more. A detective. Unobserved, he went down to his stuffy cabin, took off the chamois bag and locked it in his trunk. So long as it remained on board, it was in British territory.

The following day he went into the great city of man-made cliffs. He walked miles and miles. Naturally he sought the haberdashers along Broadway. No employment was offered him: for the reason that he failed to state his accomplishments. But he was in nowise discouraged. He would go back to Liverpool. The ship would sail with full cabin strength, and this trip there would be tips, three sovereigns at least, and maybe more, if his charges happened to be generous.

He tied the chamois bag round his neck again, and turned in. He was terribly tired and footsore. He slept fitfully. At half after nine he sat up, fully awake. His cabin-mate (whom he rather disliked) was not in his bunk. Indeed, the bunk had not been touched. Suddenly Thomas' hand flew to his breast.

The chamois bag was gone!

CHAPTER IV

Iambic and hexameter, farewell! In that moment the poet died in Thomas; I mean, the poet who had to dig his expressions of life out of ink-pots. Things boil up quickly and unexpectedly in the soul; century-old impulses, undreamed of by the inheritor; and when these bubble and spill over the kettle's lip, watch out. There is an island in the South Seas where small mud-geysers burst forth under the pressure of the foot. Fate had stepped on Thomas.

As he sprang out of his bunk he was a reversion: the outlaw in Lincoln-green, the Yeoman of the Guard, the bandannaed smuggler of the southeast coast. Quickly he got into his uniform. He went about this affair the right way, with foresight and prudence; for he realized that he must act instantly. He sought the purser, who was cordial.

"I'm not feeling well," began Thomas; "and the doctor is ashore. Where's there an apothecary's shop?"

"Two blocks straight out from the pier entrance. You'll see red and blue lights in the windows. Tummy?"

"I'm subject to dizzy spells. Where's Jameson?" Jameson was the surly cabin-mate.

"Quit. Gone over to the Cunard. Fool. Like a little money advanced? Here's a bill, five dollars."

"Thank you, sir." Twenty shillings, ten pence. "Doesn't Jameson take his peg a little too often, sir?"

"He's a blighter. Glad to get rid of him. Hurry back. And don't stop at Mike's or Johnny's," — smiling.

"I never touch anything heavier than ale, sir." Mike's or Johnny's; it saved him the trouble of asking. Tippling pubs where stewards foregathered.

His uniform was his passport. Nobody questioned him as he passed the barrier at a dog-trot. Outside the smelly pier (sugar, coffee and spices, shipments from Killigrew and Company) he paused to send a short prayer to heaven. Then he approached a snoozing stevedore.

"Where's Mike's?"

"Lead y' there, ol' scout!"

"No; tell me where it is. Here's a shilling."

Explicit directions followed; and away went Thomas at a dog-trot again: the lust to punish, maim or kill in his heart. He was not a university man; he had not played cricket at Lord's or stroked the crew from Leander; but he was island-born, a chap for cold tubbings, calisthenics and long tramps into the country on pleasant Sundays. Thomas was slender, but sound and hard.

Jameson was not at Mike's nor at Johnny's; but there were dozens of other saloons. He did not ask questions. He went in, searched, and strode out. In the lowest kind of a drinking dive he found his man. A great wave of dizziness swept over Thomas. When it passed, only the bandannaed smuggler remained, cautious, cunning, patient.

The quarry was alone in a side-room, drinking gin and smiling to himself. For an hour Thomas waited. His palms became damp with cold sweat and his knees wabbled, but not in fear. Four glasses of ale, sipped slowly, tasting of wormwood. In the bar-mirror he could watch every move made by Jameson. No one went in. He had evidently paid in advance for the bottle of gin. Thomas ordered his fifth glass of ale, and saw Jameson's head sink forward a little. Thomas' sigh almost split his heart in twain. Jameson's head went up suddenly, and with a drunken smile he reached for the bottle and poured out a stiff potion. He drank it neat.

Thomas wiped his palms on his sleeves and ordered a cigar.

"Lonesome?" asked the swart bartender. This good-looking chap was rather a puzzle to him. He wasn't waiting for anybody, and he wasn't trying to get drunk. Five ales in an hour and not a dozen words; just an ordinary Britisher who didn't know how to amuse himself in Gawd's own country.

Jameson's head fell upon his arms. With assured step Thomas walked toward the corridor which divided the so-called wine-rooms. At the end of the corridor was a door. He did not care where it led so long as it led outside this evil-smelling den. He found the room empty opposite Jameson's. He went in quietly. The shabby waiter followed him, soft-footed as a cat.

"A bottle of Old Tom," said Thomas.

The waiter nodded and slipped out. He saw the

sleeper in the other room, and gently closed the door.

"Gink in number two wants a bottle o' gin. He's th' kind. Layer o' ale an' then his quart. Th' real souse."

"So that's his game, huh?" said the bartender. "How's th' gink in number four?"

"Dead t' th' world."

"Tip th' Sneak. There may be a chancet t' roll 'em both. Here y' are. Soak 'im two-fifty."

Half an hour longer Thomas waited. Then he rose and tiptoed to the door, drawing it back without the least sound. Jameson's had not latched. Taking a deep long breath (strange, how one may control the heart by this process!) Thomas crossed the corridor and entered the other room; entered prepared for any emergency. If Jameson awoke, so much the worse for him. The gods owe it to the mortals they keep in bondage to bestow a grain of luck here and there along the way to Elysium or Hades. His cabin-mate's stentorian breathing convinced the trespasser that it was the stupidest, heaviest kind of sleep.

For a moment he looked down at the man con-temptuously. To have befuddled his brain at such a time! Or was it because the wretch knew that he, Thomas, would not dare cry out over his loss? He stepped behind the sleeping man. He wanted to fall upon him, beat him with his fists. Ah, if he had not found him!

The night, fortunately, was warm and thick.

Jameson had carelessly thrown open his coat and vest. Underneath he wore the usual sailor-jersey. Thomas steeled his arms. With one hand he pulled the roll collar away from the man's neck and with the other sought for the string: sought in vain. The light, the four drab walls, the haze of tobacco smoke, all turned red.

"Where is it, you dog? Quick!" Thomas shook the man. "Where is it? Quick, or I'll throttle you!"

"Lemme 'lone!" Jameson sagged toward the table again.

Thomas bent him back ruthlessly and plunged a hand into the inside pocket of the man's coat. The touch of the chamois-bag burned like fire. He pulled it out and transferred it to his own pocket and made for the door. He did not care now what happened. Found! Woe to any one who had the ill-luck to stand between him and the exit.

Outside the door stood the shabby waiter, grinning cheerfully. He was accompanied by a hulking, shifty-eyed creature.

"Roll 'im, ol' sport? Caught in th' act, huh?" gibed the waiter.

Thomas had the right idea. He struck first. The waiter crashed against the wall. The hulking, shifty-eyed one fared worse. He went down with his face to the cracks in the floor. Thomas dashed for the exit.

CHAPTER V

Outside he found himself in a kind of court. He ran about wildly, like a rat in a trap. He plumped into the alley, accidentally. Down this he fled, into the street. A voice called out peremptorily to him to stop, but he went on all the faster, swift as a hare. He doubled and circled through this street and that until at last he came out into a broad, brilliant thoroughfare. An iron-pillared railway reared itself skyward and trains clamored past. Bloomsbury: millions of years and miles away! He would wake up presently, with the sunlight (when it shone) pouring into his room, and the bright geraniums on the outside window-sill bidding him good morning.

He was on the point of rushing up the station stairway, when he espied a cab at the far corner. A replica of a London cab, something which smacked of home; he could have hugged for sheer joy the bleary-eyed cabby who touched his rusty high hat.

"Free?"

"Free 's th' air, bo. Where to?"

"Pier 60, White Star Line. How much?" — quite his old-time self again.

"Two dollars," — promptly.

"All right. And hurry!" Thomas climbed in. He was safe.

As the crow flies it was less than a ten-minutes' jog from that corner to Pier 60. Thomas had not gone far; he had merely covered a good deal of ground.

Cabby drove about for three-quarters of an hour and then drew up before the pier.

Back to his cabin once more, weak as a swimmer who had breasted a strong tide. He opened his trunk and rammed the chamois-bag into the toe of one of his patent-leather boots. In the daytime he would wear it about his neck, but each night back into the shoe it must go. He flung himself on the bunk, not to sleep, but to think and wonder.

Meantime there was great excitement in the dive. The waiter was rocking his body, wailing and holding his jaw. His companion was sitting on the floor. In the wine-room two policemen and a thickset, black-mustached man in a derby hat were asking questions.

"Robbed!" moaned Jameson.

The man in the derby hat shook him roughly. "Robbed o' what, y' soak?"

"Robbed!"

"Mike," said the man in the derby, "put th' darbies on th' Sneak. We'll get something for our trouble, anyhow. An' tell that waiter t' put th' brakes on his yawp. Bring him in here. Now, you, what's happened?"

"Why, the gink in uniform comes in…"

The bartender interrupted. "A gink dressed like a ship-steward comes in an' orders ale. Drinks five glasses. Goes out int' th' wine-room 'cross th' hall an' orders a bottle o' gin. An' next I hears Johnny howlin' murder. Frame-up, Mr. Haggerty. Nothin' t' do with it, hones' t' Gawd! Th' boss ain't here."

Jameson lurched toward the bartender. "Young lookin'? Red cheeks? 'Old himself like a sojer?"

"That's 'im," agreed the bartender.

"What were y' robbed of?" demanded Haggerty.

Jameson looked into a pair of chilling blue eyes. His own wavered drunkenly. "Money."

"Y' lie! What was it?" Haggerty seized Jameson by the collar and swung him about. "Hurry up!"

"I tell you, my money. Paid off t'dy. 'E knew it. Sly." Jameson had become almost sober. Out of the muddle one thing loomed clearly: he could not be revenged upon his cabin-mate without getting himself into deep trouble. Money; he'd stick to that.

"Who is he?"

"Name's Webb; firs'-class steward on th' *Celtic*. Damn 'im!"

"Lock this fool up till morning," said Haggerty. "I'll find out what he's been robbed of."

"British subject!" roared Jameson.

"Not t'night. Take 'im away. Think I saw th' fellow running as I came by. Yelled at him, but he could run some. Take 'im away. Something fishy about this. I'll call on my friend Webb in th' morning. There might be something in this."

And Haggerty paid his call promptly; only, Thomas saw him first. The morning sun lighted up the rugged Irish face. Thomas not only saw him but knew who he was, and in this he had the advantage of the encounter. One of the first things a detective has to do is to surprise his man, and then immediately begin to bullyrag and overbear him; pretend that all is known, that the game is up. Nine times out of ten it serves, for in the same ratio there is always a doubtful confederate who may "peach" in order to save himself.

Thomas never stirred from his place against the rail. He drew on his pipe and pretended to be stolidly interested in the sweating stevedores, the hoist-booms and the brown coffee-bags.

A hand fell lightly on his shoulder. Haggerty had a keen eye for a face; he saw weak spots, where a hundred other men would have seen nothing out of the ordinary. The detective always planned his campaign upon his interpretation of the face of the intended victim.

"Webb?"

Thomas lowered his pipe and turned. "Yes, sir."

"Where were you between 'leven an' twelve last night?"

"What is that to you, sir?" (Yeoman of the Guard style.)

"What did Jameson take away from you?"

"Who are you, and what's your business with me?" The pipe-stem returned with a click to its ivory vise.

"My name is Haggerty, of th' New York detective force; American Scotland Yard, 'f that'll sound better. Better tell me all about it."

"I'm a British subject, on board a British ship."

"Nothing doing in m' lord style. When y' put your foot on that pier you become amenable t' th' laws o' th' United States, especially 'f you've committed a crime."

"A crime?"

"Listen here. You went int' Lumpy Joe's, waited till Jameson got drunk, an' then you rolled him."

"Rolled?" — genuinely bewildered.

"Picked his pockets, if you want it blunt. Th' question is, did he take it from you 'r you from him? I can arrest you, Mr. Webb, British subject 'r not. 'S up t' you t' tell me th' story. Don't be afraid of me; I don't eat up men. All y' got t' do is t' treat me on th' level. You won't lose anything 'f you're honest."

"Come with me, sir." (The smuggler was, in his day, a match in cunning for any or all of His Majesty's coast-guards.)

Haggerty followed the young man down the various companionways. Instinctively he knew what was coming, the pith of the matter if not the details. Thomas pulled out his trunk, unlocked it, threw back the lid, and picked up an old leather box.

"Look at this, sir. It was my mother's. And I'd be a fine chap, would I not, to let a drunken scoundrel steal it and get away with it."

It was a Neapolitan brooch, of pink coral, sur-

39

rounded by small pearls. Haggerty balanced it on his palm and appraised it at three or found hundred dollars. He glanced casually into the leather box. Some faded tin-types, some letters, a very old Bible, and odds and ends of a young man's fancy: Haggerty shrugged. It looked as if he had stumbled into a mare's-nest.

"He said you took money."

"He lied," — tersely.

"Do y' want t' appear against him?"

"No. We sail at seven to-morrow. So long as he missed his shot, let him go."

"Why didn't y' lodge a complaint against him?"

"I'm not familiar with your laws, Mr. Haggerty. So I took the matter in my own hands."

"Don't do it again. Sorry t' trouble you. But duty's duty. An' listen. Always play your game above board; it pays."

"Thanks."

Haggerty started to offer his hand, but the look in the gray eyes caused him to misdoubt and reconsider the impulse. So Thomas made his first mistake, which, later on, was to cost him dear. Coconnas shook hands with Caboche the headsman, and escaped the "question extraordinary." Truth is, Thomas was not an accomplished liar. He could lie to the detective, but he could not bring himself to shake hands on it.

On the way down the plank Haggerty mused:

"An' I thought I had a hunch!"

Thomas sighed. "Play your game above board; it pays." Into what a labyrinth of lies he was wayfaring!

That same night, on the other side of the Atlantic, the ninth Baron of Dimbledon sailed for America to rehabilitate his fortunes. He did and he didn't.

CHAPTER VI

Thomas was a busy man up to and long after the hour of sailing. His cabins were filled with about all the variant species of the race: two nervous married women with their noisy mismanaged children, three young men on a lark, and an actress who was paying her husband's expenses and gladly announced the fact over and through the partitions. Three bells tingled all day long, and the only thing that saved Thomas from the "sickbay" was the fact that the bar closed at eleven. And a rough passage added to his labors. No Henley this voyage, no comfy loafing about the main-deck in the sunshine. A busy, miserable, dejected young man, who cursed his folly and yet clung to it with that tenacity which makes prejudice England's first-born.

Night after night, stretched out wearily on his bunk, the sordid picture of Lumpy Joe's returned to him. By a hair's breadth! It was always a source of amazement to recall how quickly and shrewdly his escape had been managed. He felt reasonably safe. Jameson would never dare tell what he knew, to incriminate himself for the sake of revenge. To have got the best of him and to have pulled the wool over the eyes of a keen American detective!

In Liverpool he deliberately threw away a full sovereign in motion-pictures and music-halls. But he drank nothing, not even his customary ale. Not so long ago he had tasted his first champagne; very expensive, something more than two hundred pounds. Stupid ass! And yet... The very life he had always been longing for, dreaming of, behind his counters: to be free, to rove at will, to seek adventure.

"Then," said Sir Tristram, "I will fight with you unto the uttermost." "I grant," said Sir Palomides, "for in a better quarrel keep I never to fight, for and I die of your hands, of a better knight's hands may I not be slain."...

Off for America again; and the Book of Marvelous Adventures, to be opened wide by a pair of Irish blue eyes, deep as the sea, glancing as the sunlight on its crests.

"You are my steward, I believe?"

In his soul of souls Thomas hoped so. "Yes, miss — indeed, yes, if you occupy this cabin."

"Here are the tickets"; and the young lady signed the slip of paper he gave her: Mr. and Mrs. Daniel Killigrew, Miss Killigrew and maid. "I shall probably keep you very busy." There was a twinkle in her eyes, but he was English and did not see it.

"That is what I am here for, miss." He smiled reassuringly.

"Never ask my father if he wishes tea and toast" — gravely.

"Yes, miss" — with honest gravity. Thomas knew nothing of women, young or old. With the habits and tastes of the male biped he was tolerably familiar. He was to learn.

"Hot water-bottles for my mother every night, and a pot of chocolate for myself. I shall always have my breakfast early in the saloon. I'm a first-rate sailor."

A rush, a whir.

"Kitty, you darling! They have put us on the other side of the ship."

Thomas was genuinely glad of it. With a goddess and a nymph to wait upon, heaven knew how many broken dishes he'd have to account for. Never in the park, never after the matinees, never in all wide London, had he seen two such lovely types: Titian and Greuse.

"No!" said the Greuse.

"Stupid mistake at the booking-office," replied the Titian. "Come up on deck. They are putting off."

"Just a moment. Put the small luggage, Mr…"

"Webb."

"Mr. Webb. Put the small luggage on the lounge. Never mind the straps. That is all."

"Yes, miss."

The two young women hurried off. Thomas stared after them, his brows bent in a mixture of perplexity, dazzlement and diffidence.

"A very good-looking steward."

"Kitty, you little wretch!"

"Why, he *is* good-looking."

"Princes, dukes, waiters, cabbies, stewards; all you do is look at them, and they become slaves.

You've more mischief in you than a dozen kittens."

"I have met cabbies whom I much prefer to certain dukes."

"But I've a young man picked out for you. He's an artist."

"Good night!" murmured Kitty. "If there is one kind of person in the world dad considers wholly useless and incompetent, it's an artist or a poet."

"But this artist makes fifteen thousand and sometimes twenty thousand the year."

"Then he's no artist. What is his name?"

"Forbes, J. Mortimer Forbes."

"Oh. The pretty-cover man."

"My dear, he is one of the nicest young men in New York. His family is one of the best, and he goes everywhere. And but for his kindness..."

"What?"

"Some day I'll tell you the story. Here we go! Good-by, England!"

"Good-by, sapphires!" said Kitty, so low that the other did not hear her.

At dinner Thomas was called to account by the chief steward for permitting his thumb to connect with the soup. But what would you, with Titian and Greuse smiling a soft "Thank you!" for everything you did for them?

*****

45

"Night, daddy."

"Good night, Kittibudget."

Crawford smiled after the blithe, buoyant figure as it swung confidently down the deck.

"I don't know what I'm going to do," mused Killigrew, looking across the rail at the careening stars.

"What about?"

"That child. I can't harness her."

"Somebody's bound to" — prophetically.

"It's got to be a whole man, or he'll wish he'd never been born. She's had her way so long that she's spoiled."

"Not a bit of it."

"Yes, she is. I told her not to wear those sapphires that night. And, by the way, I've been hoping they'd turn up like that ruby of yours. How do you account for that?"

The coal of Crawford's cigar waxed and waned and the ash lengthened.

"I've no doubt that you've been mighty curious since that morning. Perhaps you read the tale in the newspapers. I know of only one man who would return the Nana Sahib's ruby. Sentiment; for I believe the poor devil was really fond of me. A valet. With me for ten years. He was really my comrade; always my right-hand on my exploration trips; back-boned, fearless, reliable in a pinch, and a scholar in a way; though I can't imagine how and where he picked up his learning. He saved my life at least twice by his quick wit. In those days I was something of a stick; never went out. I hired him upon his word and because he looked honest. And he was for ten years. He gave his name as Mason, said he was born in central New York. We got along without friction of any sort. And I still miss him. Stole a hundred thousand dollars' worth of gems; hid them in the heels of my old shoes and nearly got away with them. Haggerty, the detective, thought for weeks that I was the man. I still believe that I was the innocent cause of Mason's relapse; for Haggerty was certain that somewhere in the past Mason had been a criminal. You see, I had a peculiar fad. I used to buy up old safes and open them for the sport of it. Crazy idea, but I found a good deal of amusement in it."

"You don't say!" gasped Killigrew, who had never heard of this phase before.

"It's my belief that Mason got his inspiration from watching me. I am devilish sorry."

"Then you believe that he is up to his old tricks again?"

"Yes," — reluctantly. "The man who took my wife's ruby, took your daughter's sapphires. It needed a clever mind to conceive such a *coup*. Three other carriages were entered, with more or less success. In a dense fog; a needle in a haystack. And they'll never find him."

"It's up to you to put the detectives on the right track."

"I suppose I'll have to do it."

"If he returns to America he'll be caught. I'll give Haggerty the tip."

"I have my doubts of Mason committing any such folly. He picked up a small fortune that night. Strange mix-up."

"Here, try one of these," urged Killigrew, as the butt of Crawford's cigar went overboard.

"Thanks."

Thomas moved away from the ventilator. Mix-up, indeed! He stole down to the promenade deck, where the stewardess informed him that Miss Killigrew had just ordered her chocolate. He flew to the kitchens. It was a narrow escape. To have been found wanting the first night out!

"Come in," said a voice in answer to his knock.

"Come in," said a voice

"Come in," said a voice.

He set the tray down on the stool, his heart insurgent and his fingers all thumbs. He might live to be a steward eighty years old, but he never would get over the awe, the embarrassment of these invasions by night. Each time he saw a woman in her peignoir or kimono he felt as though he had committed a sacrilege. True, he understood their attitude; he was merely a serving machine and for the time wiped off the roster of mankind.

A long blue coat of silk brocade enveloped Kitty from her throat to her sandals; sleeves which fell over her hands; buttoned by loops over corded knots. An experienced traveler could have told him that it was the peculiar garment which any self-respecting Chinaman would wear who was in mourning for his grandfather. Kitty wore it because of its beauty alone.

"Thank you," she said, as Thomas went out backward, court style. Kitty smiled across at her maid who was arranging the combs and brushes preparatory to taking down her mistress' hair. "He looked as if he were afraid of something, Celeste."

Celeste smiled enigmatically. "Ma'm'selle shoult haff been born in Pariss."

This was translatable, or not, as you pleased. Kitty sipped the chocolate and found it excellent. At length she dismissed the maid, switched off the lights, and then remembered that there was no water in the carafe. She rang.

Thomas replied so promptly that he could not have been farther off than the companionway. "You rang, miss?"

"Yes, Webb. Please fill this carafe."

"Is it possible that it was empty, miss?"

"I used it and forgot to ring for more."

All this in the dark.

Thomas hurried away, wishing he could find some magic spring on board. For what purpose he could not have told.

As for Kitty, she remained standing by the door, profoundly astonished.

CHAPTER VII

Third day out.

Kitty smiled at the galloping horizon; smiled at the sunny sky; smiled at the deck-steward as he served the refreshing broth; smiled at the tips of her sensible shoes, at her hands, at her neighbors: until Mrs. Crawford could contain her curiosity no longer.

"Kitty Killigrew, what have you been doing?"

"Doing?"

"Well, going to do?" — shrewdly.

Kitty gazed at her friend in pained surprise, her blue eyes as innocent as the sea — and as full of hidden mysterious things. "Good gracious! can't a person be happy and smile?"

"Happy I have no doubt you are; but I've studied that smile of yours too closely not to be alarmed by it."

"Well, what does it say?"

"Mischief."

Kitty did not reply to this, but continued smiling — at space this time.

On the ship crossing to Naples in February their chairs on deck had been together; they had become acquainted, and this acquaintance had now ripened into one of those intimate friendships which are really sounder and more lasting than those formed in youth. Crawford had heard of Killigrew as a great and prosperous merchant, and Killigrew had heard of Crawford as a millionaire whose name was very rarely mentioned in the society pages of the Sunday newspapers. Men recognize men at once; it doesn't take much digging. Before they arrived in Naples they had agreed to take the Sicilian trip together, then up Italy, through France, to England. The scholar and the merchant at play were like two boys out of school; the dry whimsical humor of the Scotsman and the volatile sparkle of the Irishman made them capital foils.

Killigrew dropped his *Rodney Stone*.

"Say, Crawford," he began, "after seeing ten thousand saints in ten thousand cathedrals, since February, I'd give a hundred dollars for a ringside ticket to a scrap like that one," — indicating the volume on his knee.

Crawford lay back and laughed.

"Well," said his wife, with an amused smile, "why don't you say it?"

"Say what?"

"'So would I!'"

"Men are quite hopeless," sighed Mrs. Killigrew, when the laughter had subsided.

"You oughtn't object to a good shindy, Molly," slyly observed her husband. "You'll never forgive me that black eye."

"I'll never forgive the country you got it in," — grimly. "But what's the harm in a good scrap between two husky fellows, trained to a hair to slam-bang each other?"

"It isn't refined, dad," said Kitty.

He sent a searching glance at her; he never was sure when that girl was laughing. "Fiddle-sticks! For four months now I've been shopping every day with you women, and you can't tell me prize-fights are brutal."

Crawford applauded gently.

"By the way, Crawford, you know something about direct charity." Killigrew threw back his rug and sat up. "I've got an idea. What's the use of giving checks to hospitals and asylums and colleges, when you don't know whether the cash goes right or wrong? I'm going to let Molly here start a home-bureau to keep her from voting; a lump sum every year to give away as she pleases. I'm strong for giving boys college education. Smooths 'em out; gives them a start in life; that is, if they are worth anything at the beginning. Like this: back the boy and screw up his honor and interest by telling him that you expect to be paid back when the time comes. There's no better charity in the world than making a man of a boy, making him want to stand on his own feet, independent. When you help inefficient people, you throw your money away. What do you think of the idea?"

"A first-rate one. I'd like to come in."

"No; this is all my own and Molly's. But how'll I start her off?"

"Get an efficient young man to act as private

secretary; a fairly good accountant; no rich man's son, but some one who has had a chance to observe life. Make him a buffer between Mrs. Killigrew and the whining cheats. And above all, no young man who has social entrée to your house. That kind of a private secretary is always a fizzle."

"Any one in mind?"

"No."

"I have," said Kitty, rising and going toward the companion-ladder to the lower decks.

"What now?" demanded Killigrew.

"Let her be; Kitty has a sensible head on her shoulders, for all her foolery." Mrs. Killigrew laid a restraining hand on her husband's arm.

But Mrs. Crawford smiled a replica of that smile which had aroused her curiosity in regard to Kitty. And then her face grew serious.

Kitty had a mind like her father's. Her ideas were seldom nebulous or slow in forming. They sprang forth, full grown, like those mythological creatures: Minerva was an idea of Jove's, as doubtless Venus was an idea of Neptune's. Men with this quality become captains-general of armies or of money-bags. In a man it signifies force; in a woman, charm.

Kitty searched diligently and found the object of her quest on the main-deck, starboard, leaning against one of the deck supports and reading from a book which lay flat on the broad teak rail, in a blue shadow. The sea smiled at Kitty and Kitty smiled at the sea. Men are not the only adventurers; they have no monopoly on daring. And what Kitty proposed doing was daring indeed, for she did not know into what dangers it might eventually lead her.

"Mr. Webb?"

Thomas looked up. "You are wanting me, miss?"

"If you are not too busy."

"Really, no. I have been reading." He closed the book, loose-leafed from frequent perusals. "I am at your service."

"Do you read much, Mr. Webb?"

The reiteration of the prefix to his name awakened him to the marvelous fact that for the present he was no longer the machine; she was recognizing the man.

"Perhaps, for a man in my station, I read too much, Miss Killigrew."

Kitty's scarlet lips stirred ever so slightly. It was the first time he had added the name to the prefix: he in his turn was recognizing the woman. And this rather pleased her, for she liked to be recognized.

"May I ask what it is you are reading?"

He offered the book to her. *Morte d'Arthur.* Kitty's eyebrows, a hundred years or more ago, would have stirred to tender lyrics the quills of Prior and Lovelace and Suckling: arched when interested, a funny little twist to the inner points when angered, and when laughter possessed her... Let Thomas indite the sonnet! Just now they were widely arched.

"I am very fond of the book," explained Thomas diffidently. "I love the pompous gallantry of these fairy chaps. How politely they used to hack each other into pieces!"

"Are you by chance a university man?"

"No. I am self-educated, if one may call it that. My father was a fellow at Trinity. For myself, I have always had to work."

"Do you like your present occupation?"

"It was the best I could find." How he would have liked to throw discretion to the winds and tell her the whole miserable story!

"Are you good at accounting?"

"Fairly." What was all this about? He began to riffle the leaves of the book, restively.

"Could you tell an honest man from a dishonest one?"

"I believe so." Thomas had eyebrows, too, but he did not know how to use them properly. Tell an honest man from a dishonest one, forsooth!

Kitty found the situation less easy than she had anticipated. The more questions she asked, the more embarrassed she grew; and it angered her because there was no clear reason why she should become embarrassed. And she also remarked his uneasiness. However, she went on determinedly.

"Have you ever had any contact with real poverty?"

"Yes," — close-lipped. "Pardon me, Miss Killigrew, but..."

"Just a moment, Mr. Webb," she interrupted. "I dare say my questions seem impertinent, but they have a purpose back of them. My mother and I are looking for a private secretary for a charitable concern which we are going to organize shortly. We desire some one who is educated, who will be capable of guarding us from persons not worthy of benefactions, who will make recommendations, seek into the affairs of those considered worthy. We shall, of course, expect to find room for you. It will not be a chatter-tea-drinking affair. You will have the evenings to yourself and all of Sundays. The salary will be two hundred a month."

"Pounds?" gasped Thomas.

"Oh, no; dollars. I do not expect your answer at this moment. You must have time to think it over."

"It is not necessary, Miss Killigrew."

"You decline?"

"On the contrary, I accept with a good deal of gratitude. On condition," he added gravely.

"And that?"

"You will ask me no questions regarding my past."

Kitty looked squarely into his eyes and he returned the glance steadily and calmly.

"Very well; I accept the condition,"

Thomas was mightily surprised.

CHAPTER VIII

He had put forward this condition, perfectly sure that she would refuse to accept it. He could not understand.

"You accept that condition?"

"Yes." Having gone thus far with her plot, Kitty would have died rather than retreated; Irish temperament.

Thomas was moved to a burst of confidence. "I know that I am poor, and to the best of my belief, honest. Moreover, perhaps I should be compelled by the exigencies of circumstance to leave you after a few months. I am not a rich man, masquerading for the sport of it; I am really poor and grateful for any work. It is only fair that I should tell you this much, that I am running away from no one. Beyond the fact that I am the son of a very great but unknown scholar, a farmer of mediocre talents who lost his farm because he dreamed of humanity instead of cabbages, I have nothing to say." He said it gravely, without pride or veiled hauteur.

"That is frank enough," replied Kitty, curiously stirred. "You will not find us hard task-masters. Be here this afternoon at three. My father will wish to talk to you. And be as frank with him as you have been with me."

She smiled and nodded brightly, and turned away. He had a glimpse of a tan shoe and a slim tan-silk ankle, which poised birdlike above the high doorsill; and then she vanished into the black shadow of the companionway. She afterward confessed to me that her sensation must have been akin to that of a boy who had stolen an apple and beaten the farmer in the race to the road.

We all make the mistake of searching for our drama, forgetting that it arrives sooner or later, unsolicited.

Bewitched. Thomas should have been the happiest man alive, but the devil had recruited him for his miserables. Her piquant face no longer confronting and bewildering him, he saw this second net into which he had permitted himself to be drawn. As if the first had not been colossal enough! Where would it all end? Private secretary and two hundred the month — forty pounds — this was a godsend. But to take her orders day by day, to see her, to be near her... Poverty-stricken wretch that he was, he should have declined. Now he could not; being a simple Englishman, he had given his word and meant to abide by it. There was one glimmer of hope; her father. He was a practical merchant and would not permit a man without a past (often worse than a man with one) to enter his establishment.

Thomas was not in love with Kitty. (Indeed, this isn't a love story at all.) Stewards, three days out, are not in the habit of falling in love with their charges (Maundering and Drool notwithstanding). He was afraid of her; she vaguely alarmed him; that was all.

For seven years he had dwelt in his "third floor back"; had breakfasted and dined with two old maids, their scrawny niece, and a muscular young stenographer who shouted militant suffrage and was not above throwing a brickbat whenever the occasion arrived. There was a barmaid or two at the pub where he lunched at noon; but chaff was the alpha and omega of this acquaintance. Thus, Thomas knew little or nothing of the sex.

The women with whom he conversed, played the gallant, the hero, the lover (we none of us fancy ourselves as rogues!) were those who peopled his waking dreams. She was La Belle Isoude, Elaine, Beatrice, Constance; it all depended upon what book he had previously been reading. It is when we men are confronted with the living picture of some one of our dreams of them that women cease to dwell in the abstract and become issues, to be met with more or less trepidation. Back among some of his idle dreams there had been a Kitty, blue-eyed, black-haired, slender and elfish.

Kitty sat down in her chair. "Well," she said, "I have found him."

"Found whom?" asked Mrs. Crawford.

"The private secretary."

"What?" Killigrew swung his feet to the deck. "What the dickens have you been doing now? Who is it?"

"Webb."

"The steward?"

"Yes."

"Well, if that…" began Killigrew belligerently.

"Dad, either mother and I act as we please, or

you may attend to the home-bureau yourself. Mother, it was agreed and understood that I should select any employee we might happen to need."

"It was, my dear."

"Very good. I want some one who will attend to the affairs honestly and painstakingly. There must be no idler about the house; and any young man..."

"Wouldn't an old one do?" suggested Killigrew.

"Whose set ideas would clash constantly with ours. And any young man we know would idle and look on the whole affair as a fine joke. I've had a talk with Webb. He's not a university man, but he's educated. I found him reading *Morte d'Arthur*."

"Ah!" — from Crawford.

"He became a steward because he could find nothing else to do at the present time. He has been poor, and I dare say he has known the pinch of poverty. You said only this morning, dad, that he was the most attentive steward you had ever met on shipboard. Besides, there is a case in point. Our butler was a steward before you engaged him, six years ago."

Killigrew began to smile. "How much have you offered him as a salary?"

"Two hundred a month, to be paid out of the funds."

"Janet," said Crawford, "it's a good thing I'm married, or I'd apply for the post myself."

"All right," agreed Killigrew; "a bargain's a bargain."

"A wager's a wager," thought Kitty.

"If you wake up some fine morning and find the funds gone…"

"Mother and I will attend to all checks, such as they are."

"Kitty, any day you say I'll take you into the firm as chief counsel. But before I approve of your selection, I'd like to have a talk with our friend Webb."

"He expects it. You are to see him on the main-deck at three this afternoon."

"Molly, how long have we been married?"

"Thirty years, Daniel."

"How old is Kitty?"

"Mother!"

"Twenty-two," answered Mrs. Killigrew relent-lessly.

"Well, I was going to say that I've learned more about the Killigrew family in these four months of travel than in all those years together."

"Something more than ornaments," suggested Kitty dryly.

"Yes, indeed," replied her father amiably.

And when he returned to the boat-deck that af-ternoon for tea (which, by the way, he never drank, being a thorough-going coffee merchant), he said to

Kitty: "You win on points. If Webb doesn't pan out, why, we can discharge him. I'll take a chance at a man who isn't afraid to look you squarely in the eyes."

At the precise time when Kitty retired and Thomas went aft for his good night pipe — eleven o'clock at sea and nine in New York — Haggerty found himself staring across the street at an old-fashioned house. Like the fisherman who always returns to the spot where he lost the big one, the detective felt himself drawn toward this particular dwelling. Crawford did not live there any more; since his marriage he had converted it into a private museum. It was filled with mummies and carton-nages, ancient pottery and trinkets.

What a game it had been! A hundred thousand in precious gems, all neatly packed away in the heels of Crawford's old shoes! And where was that man Mason? Would he ever return? Oh, well; he, Haggerty, had got his seven thousand in rewards; he was living now like a nabob up in the Bronx. He had no real cause to regret Mason's advent or his escape. Yet, deep in his heart burned the chagrin of defeat: his man had got away, and half the game (if you're a true hunter) was in putting your hand on a man's shoulder and telling him to "Come along."

He crossed the street and entered the, alley and gazed up at the fire-escape down which Mason had made his escape. What impelled the detective to leap up and catch the lower bars of the ground-ladder he could not have told you. He pulled himself up and climbed to the window.

Open!

Haggerty had nerves like steel wires, but a slight shiver ran down his spine. Open, and Crawford yet on the high seas. He waited, listening intently. Not a sound of any sort came to his ears. He stepped inside courageously and slipped with his back to the wall, where he waited, holding his breath.

Click! It seemed to come from his right.

"Come out o' that!" he snarled. "No monkey-business, or I'll shoot."

He flashed his pocket-lamp toward the sound, and aimed.

A blow on the side of the head sent the detective crashing against a cartonnage, and together the quick and the dead rolled to the floor. Instinctively Haggerty turned on his back, aimed at the window and fired.

Too late!

CHAPTER IX

When the constellation, which was not included among the accepted theories of Copernicus, passed away, Haggerty sat up and rubbed the swelling over his ear, tenderly yet grimly. Next, he felt about the floor for his pocket-lamp. A strange spicy dust drifted into his nose and throat, making him sneeze and cough. A mummy had reposed in the over-turned cartonnage and the brittle bindings had crumbled into powder. He soon found the lamp, and sent its point of vivid white light here and there about the large room.

Pursuit of his assailant was out of the question. Haggerty was not only hard of head but shrewd. So he set about the accomplishment of the second best course, that of minute and particular investigation. Some one had entered this deserted house: for what? This, Haggerty must find out. He was fairly confident that the intruder did not know who had challenged him; on the other hand, there might be lying around some clue to the stranger's identity.

Was there light in the house, fluid in the wires? If so he would be saved the annoyance of exploring the house by the rather futile aid of the pocket-lamp, which stood in need of a fresh battery. He searched for the light-button and pressed it, hopefully. The room, with all its brilliantly decorated antiquities, older than Rome, older than Greece, blinded Haggerty for a space. "Ain't that like these book chaps?" Haggerty murmured. "T' go away without turning off th' meter!"

The first thing Haggerty did was to scrutinize the desk which stood near the center of the room. A film of dust lay upon it. Not a mark anywhere. In fact, a quarter of an hour's examination proved to Haggerty's mind that nothing in this room had been disturbed except the poor old mummy. He concluded to leave that gruesome object where it lay. Nobody but Crawford would know how to put him back in his box, poor devil. Haggerty wondered if, after a thousand years, some one would dig him up!

Through all the rooms on this floor he prowled, but found nothing. He then turned his attention to the flight of stairs which led to the servants' quarters. Upon the newel-post lay the fresh imprint of a hand. Haggerty went up the stairs in bounds. There were nine rooms on this floor, two connecting with baths. In one of these latter rooms he saw a trunk, opened, its contents carelessly scattered about the floor. One by one he examined the garments, his heart beating quickly. Not a particle of dust on them; plenty of finger-prints on the trunk. It had been opened this very night — by one familiar, either at first-hand or by instruction. He had come for something in that trunk. What?

From garret to cellar, thirty rooms in all; nothing but the hand-print on the newel-post and the opened trunk. Haggerty returned to the museum, turned out all the lights except that on the desk, and sat down on a rug so as not to disturb the dust on the chairs. The man might return. It was certain that he, Haggerty, would come back on the morrow. He was anxious to compare the thumb-print with the one he had in his collection.

For what had the man come? Keep-sakes? Haggerty dearly wanted to believe that the intruder was the one man he desired in his net; but he refused to listen to the insidious whisperings; he must have proof, positive, absolute, incontestable. If it was Crawford's man Mason, it was almost too good to be true; and he did not care to court ultimate disappointment.

Proof, proof; but where? Why had the man not returned the clothes to the trunk and shut it? What had alarmed him? Everything else indicated the utmost caution... A glint of light flashing and winking from steel. Haggerty rose and went over to the window. He picked up a bunch of keys, thirty or forty in all, on a ring, weighing a good pound. The detective touched the throbbing bump and sensed a moisture; blood. So this was the weapon? He weighed the keys on his palm. A long time since he had seen a finer collection of skeleton keys, thin and flat and thick and short, smooth and notched, each a gem of its kind. Three or four ordinary keys were sandwiched in between, and Haggerty inspected these curiously.

"H'm. Mebbe it's a hunch. Anyhow, I'll try it. Can't lose anything trying."

He turned out the desk light and went down to the lower hall, his pocket-lamp serving as guide. He unlatched the heavy door-chains, opened the doors and closed them behind him. He inserted one of the ordinary keys. It refused to work. He tried another. The door swung open, easily.

"Now, then, come down out o' that!" growled a

voice at the foot of the steps. "Thought y'd be comin' out by-'n-by. No foolin' now, 'r I blow a hole through ye!"

Haggerty wheeled quickly. "'S that you, Dorgan? Come up."

"Haggerty?" said the astonished patrolman. "An' Mitchell an' I've been watchin' these lights fer an hour!"

"Some one's been here, though; so y' weren't wasting your time. I climbed up th' fire-escape in th' alley an' got a nice biff on th' coco for me pains. See any one running before y' saw th' lights?"

"Why, yes!"

"Ha! It's hard work t' get it int' your heads that when y' see a man running at this time o' night, in a quiet side-street it's up t' you t' ask him questions."

"Thought he was chasin' a cab."

"Well, listen here. Till th' owner comes back, keep your eyes peeled on this place. An' any one y' see prowling around, nab him an' send for me. On your way!"

Haggerty departed in a hurry. He had already made up his mind as to what he was going to do. He hunted up a taxicab and told the chauffeur where to go, advising him to "hit it up." His destination was the studio-apartment of J. Mortimer Forbes, the artist. It was late, but this fact did not trouble Haggerty. Forbes never went to bed until there was positively nothing else to do.

The elevator-boy informed Haggerty that Mr. Forbes had just returned from the theater. Alone? Yes. Haggerty pushed the bell-button. A dog bayed.

"Why, Haggerty, what's up? Come on in. Be still, Fritz!"

The dachel's growl ended in a friendly snuffle, and he began to dance upon Haggerty's broad-toed shoes.

"Bottle of beer? Cigar? Take that easy chair. What's on your mind tonight?" Forbes rattled away. "Why, man, there's a cut on the side of your head!"

"Uhuh. Got any witch-hazel?" The detective sat down, stretched out his legs, and pulled the dachel's ears.

Forbes ran into the bathroom to fetch the witch-hazel. Haggerty poured a little into his palm and dabbled the wound with it.

"Now, spin it out; tell me what's happened," said Forbes, filling his calabash and pushing the cigars across the table.

For a year and a half these two men, the antitheses of each other, had been intimate friends. This liking was genuine, based on secret admiration, as yet to be confessed openly. Forbes had always been drawn toward this man-hunting business; he yearned to rescue the innocent and punish the guilty. Whenever a great crime was committed he instantly overflowed with theories as to what the criminal was likely to do afterward. Haggerty enjoyed listening to his patter; and often there were illuminating flashes which obtained results for the detective, who never applied his energies in the direction of logical deduction. Besides, the chairs in the studio were comfortable, the imported beer not too cold, and the cigars beyond criticism.

Haggerty accepted a cigar, lighted it, and amusedly watched the eager handsome face of the artist.

"Any poker lately?"

"No; cut it out for six months. Come on, now; don't keep me waiting any longer."

"Mum's th' word?" — tantalizingly.

"You ought to know that by this time" — aggrieved.

Haggerty tossed the bunch of keys on the table.

"Ha! Good specimens, these," Forbes declared, handling them. "Here's a window-opener."

"Good boy!" said Haggerty, as a teacher would have commended a bright pupil.

"And a door-chain lifter. Nothing lacking. Did he hit you with these?"

"Ye-up."

"What are these regular keys for?"

"One o' them unlocks a door." Haggerty smoked luxuriously.

Forbes eyed the ordinary keys with more interest than the burglarious ones. Haggerty was presently astonished to see the artist produce his own key-ring.

"What now?"

"When Crawford went abroad he left a key with me. I am making some drawings for an Egyptian romance and wanted to get some atmosphere."

"Uhuh."

"Which key is it that unlocks a door?" asked Forbes, his eyes sparkling.

"Never'll get that out o' your head, will you?"

"Which key?"

"Th' round-headed one."

Forbes drew the key aside and laid it evenly against the one Crawford had left in his keeping.

"By George!"

"What's th' matter?"

"He's come back!" — in a whisper.

"You're a keen one! Ye-up; Crawford's valet Mason is visiting in town."

CHAPTER X

There are many threads and many knots in a net; these can not be thrown together haphazard, lest the big fish slip through. At the bottom of the net is a small steel ring, and here the many threads and the many knots finally meet. Forbes and Haggerty (who, by the way, thinks I'm a huge joke as a novelist) and the young man named Webb recounted this tale to me by threads and knots. The ring was of Kitty Killigrew, for Kitty Killigrew, by Kitty Killigrew, to paraphrase a famous line.

At one of the quieter hotels — much patronized by touring Englishmen — there was registered James Thornden and man. Every afternoon Mr. Thornden and his man rode about town in a rented touring car. The man would bundle his master's knees in a rug and take the seat at the chauffeur's side, and from there direct the journey. Generally they drove through the park, up and down Riverside, and back to the hotel in time for tea. Mr. Thornden drank tea for breakfast along with his bacon and eggs, and at luncheon with his lamb or mutton chops, and at five o'clock with especially baked muffins and apple-tarts.

Mr. Thornden never gave orders personally; his man always attended to that. The master would, early each morning, outline the day's work, and the man would see to it that these instructions were fulfilled to the letter. He was an excellent servant, by the way, light of foot, low of voice, serious of face, with a pair of eyes which I may liken to nothing so well as to a set of acetylene blow-pipes — bored right through you.

The master was middle-aged, about the same height and weight as his valet. He wore a full dark beard, something after the style of the early eighties of last century. His was also a serious countenance, tanned, dignified too; but his eyes were no match for his valet's; too dreamy, introspective. Screwed in his left eye was a monocle down from which flowed a broad ribbon. In public he always wore it; no one about the hotel had as yet seen him without it, and he had been a guest there for more than a fortnight.

He drank nothing in the way of liquor, though his man occasionally wandered into the bar and ordered a stout or an ale. After dinner the valet's time appeared to be his own; for he went out nearly every night. He seemed very much interested in shop-windows, especially those which were filled with curios. Mr. Thornden frequently went to the theater, but invariably alone.

Thus, they attracted little or no attention among the clerks and bell boys and waiters who had, in the course of the year, waited upon the wants of a royal duke and a grand duke, to say nothing of a maharajah, who was still at the hotel. An ordinary touring Englishman was, then, nothing more than that.

Until one day a newspaper reporter glanced carelessly through the hotel register. The only thing which escapes the newspaper man is the art of saving; otherwise he is omnipotent. He sees things, anticipates events, and often prearranges them; smells war if the secretary of the navy is seen to run for a street-car, is intimately acquainted with "the official in the position to know" and "the man higher up," "the gentleman on the inside," and other anonymous but famous individuals. He is tireless, impervious to rebuff, also relentless; as an investigator of crime he is the keenest hound of them all; often he does more than expose, he prevents. He is the Warwick of modern times; he makes and unmakes kings, sceptral and financial.

This particular reporter sent his card up to Mr. Thornden and was, after half an hour's delay, admitted to the suite. Mr. Thornden laid aside his tea-cup.

"I am a newspaper man, Mr. Thornden," said the young man, his eye roving about the room, visualizing everything, from the slices of lemon to the brilliant eyes of the valet.

"Ah! a pressman. What will you be wanting to see me about, sir?" — neither hostile nor friendly.

"Do you intend to remain long in America — incog?"

"Incog!" Mr. Thorndon leaned forward in his chair and drew down his eyebrow tightly against the rim of his monocle.

"Yes, sir. I take it that you are Lord Henry Monckton, ninth Baron of Dimbledon."

Master and man exchanged a rapid glance.

"Tibbets," said the master coldly, "you registered."

"Yes, sir."

"What did you register?"

"Oh," interposed the reporter, "it was the name Dimbledon caught my eye, sir. You see, there was a paragraph in one of our London exchanges that you had sailed for America. I'm what we call a hotel reporter; hunt up prominent and interesting people for interviews. I'm sure yours is a very interesting story, sir." The reporter was a pleasant, affable young man, and that was why he was so particularly efficient in his chosen line of work.

"I was not prepared to disclose my identity so soon," said Lord Monckton ruefully. "But since you have stumbled upon the truth, it is far better that I give you the facts as they are. Interviewing is a novel experience. What do you wish to know, sir?"

And thus it was that, next morning, New York — and the continent as well — learned that Lord Henry Monckton, ninth Baron of Dimbledon, had arrived in America on a pleasure trip. The story read more like the scenario of a romantic novel than a page from life. For years the eighth Baron of Dimbledon had lived in seclusion, practically forgotten. In India he had a bachelor brother, a son and a grandson. One day he was notified of the death (by bubonic plague) of these three male members of his family, the baron himself collapsed and died shortly after. The title and estate went to another branch of the family. A hundred years before, a daughter of the house had run away with the head-gardener and been disowned. The great-great-grand-son of this woman became the ninth baron. The present baron's life was recounted in full; and an adventurous life it had been, if the reporter was to be relied upon. The interview appeared in a London journal, with the single comment — "How those American reporters misrepresent things!"

It made capital reading, however; and in servants' halls the newspaper became very popular. It gave rise to a satirical leader on the editorial page: "What's the matter with us republicans? Liberty, fraternity and equality; we flaunt that flag as much as we ever did. Yet, what a howdy-do when a title comes along! What a craning of necks, what a ko-towing! How many earldoms and dukedoms are not based upon some detestable action, some despicable service rendered some orgiastic sovereign! The most honorable thing about the so-called nobility is generally the box-hedge which surrounds the manse. Kotow; pour our millions into the bottomless purses of spendthrifts; give them our most beautiful women. There is no remedy for human nature."

It was this editorial which interested Killigrew far more than the story which had given birth to it.

"That's the way to shout."

"Does it do any good?" asked Kitty. "If we had a lord for breakfast — I mean, at breakfast — would you feel at ease? Wouldn't you be watching and wondering what it was that made him your social superior?"

"Social superior? Bah!"

"That's no argument. As this editor wisely says, there's no remedy for human nature. When I was a silly schoolgirl I often wondered if there wasn't a duke in the family, or even a knight. How do you account for that feeling?"

"You were probably reading Bertha M. Clay," retorted her father, only too glad of such an opening.

"What is your opinion of titles, Mr. Webb?" she asked calmly.

"Mr. Webb is an Englishman, Kitty," reminded her mother.

"All the more reason for wishing his point of view," was the reply.

"A title, if managed well, is a fine business asset." Thomas stared gravely at his egg-cup.

"A humorist!" cried Killigrew, as if he had discovered a dodo.

"Really, no. I am typically English, sir." But Thomas was smiling this time; and when he smiled Kitty found him very attractive. She was leaning on her elbows, her folded hands propping her chin; and in his soul Thomas knew that she was looking at him with those boring critical blue eyes of hers. Why was she always looking at him like that? "It is notorious that we English are dull and stupid," he said.

"Now you are making fun of us," said Kitty seriously.

"I beg your pardon!"

She dropped her hands from under her chin and laughed. "Do you really wish to know the real secret of our antagonism, Mr. Webb?"

"I should be very glad."

"Well, then, we each of us wear a chip on our

shoulder, simply because we've never taken the trouble to know each other well. Most English we Americans meet are stupid and caddish and uninteresting; and most of the Americans you see are boastful, loud-talking and money-mad. Our mutual impressions are wholly wrong to begin with."

"I have no chip on my shoulder," Thomas refuted eagerly.

"Neither have I."

"But I have," laughed her father. "I eat Englishmen for breakfast; fe-fo-fum style."

How democratic indeed these kindly, unpretentious people were! thought Thomas. A multimillionaire as amiable as a clerk; a daughter who would have graced any court in Europe with her charm and elfin beauty. Up to a month ago he had held all Americans in tolerant contempt.

It was as Kitty said: the real Englishman and the real American seldom met.

He did not realize as yet that his position in this house was unique. In England all great merchants and statesmen and nobles had one or more private secretaries about. He believed it to be a matter of course that Americans followed the same custom. He would have been wonderfully astonished to learn that in all this mighty throbbing city of millions — people and money — there might be less than a baker's dozen who occupied simultaneously the positions of private secretary and friend of the family. Mr. Killigrew had his private secretary, but this gentleman rarely saw the inside of the Killigrew home; it wasn't at all necessary that he should. Killigrew was a sensible man; his business hours began when he left home and ended when he entered it.

"Do you know any earls or dukes?" asked Killigrew, folding his napkin.

"Really, no. I have moved in a very different orbit. I know many of them by sight, however." He did not think it vital to add that he had often sold them collars and suspenders.

The butler and the second man pulled back the ladies' chairs. Killigrew hurried away to his offices; Kitty and her mother went up-stairs; and Thomas returned to his desk in the library. He was being watched by Kitty; nothing overt, nothing tangible, yet he sensed it: from the first day he had entered this house. It oppressed him, like a presage of disaster. Back of his chair was a fireplace, above this, a mirror. Once — it was but yesterday — while with his back to his desk, day-dreaming, he had seen her in the mirror. She stood in the doorway, a hand resting lightly against the portiere. There was no smile on her face. The moment he stirred, she vanished.

Watched. Why?

CHAPTER XI

The home-bureau of charities was a success from the start; but beyond the fact that it served to establish Thomas Webb as private secretary in the Killigrew family, I was not deeply interested. I know that Thomas ran about a good deal, delving into tenements and pedigrees, judging candidates, passing or condemning, and that he earned his salary, munificent as it appeared to him. Forbes told me that he wouldn't have done the work for a thousand a week; and Forbes, like Panurge, had ten ways of making money and twelve ways of spending it.

The amazing characteristic about Thomas was his unaffected modesty, his naturalness, his eagerness to learn, his willingness to accept suggestions, no matter from what source. Haberdashers' clerks — at least, those I have known — are superior persons; they know it all, you can not tell them a single thing. I can call to witness dozens of neckties and shirts I shall never dare wear in public. But perhaps seven years among a clientele of earls and dukes, who were set in their ideas, had something to do with Thomas' attitude.

Killigrew was very well satisfied with the venture. He had had some doubts at the beginning: a man whose past ended at Pier 60 did not look like a wise speculation, especially in a household. But quite unconsciously Thomas himself had taken these doubts out of Killigrew's mind and — mislaid them. The subscriptions to all the suffragette weeklies and monthlies were dropped; and there were no more banners reading "Votes for Women" tacked over the doorways. Besides this, the merchant had a man to talk to, after dinner, he with his cigar and Thomas with his pipe, this privilege being insisted upon by the women folk, who had tact to leave the two men to themselves.

Thomas amused the millionaire. Here was a young man of a species with whom he had not come into contact in many years: a boy who did not know the first thing about poker, or bridge, or pinochle, who played outrageous billiards and who did not know who the latest reigning theatrical beauty was, and moreover, did not care a rap; who could understand a joke within reasonable time if he couldn't tell one; who was neither a nincompoop nor a molly-coddle. Thomas interested Killigrew more and more as the days went past. Happily, the voice of conscience is heard by no ears but one's own.

After luncheons Thomas had a good deal of time on his hands; and, to occupy this time he returned to his old love, composition. He began to rewrite his romance; and one day Kitty discovered him pegging away at it. He rose from his chair instantly.

"Will you be wanting me, Miss Killigrew?"

"Only to say that father will be detained downtown to-night and that you will be expected to take mother and me to the theater. It is one of your English musical comedies; and very good, they say."

Thomas had been dreading such a situation. As yet there had been no entertaining at the Killigrew home; nearly all their friends were out of town for the summer; thus far he had escaped.

"I am sorry, Miss Killigrew, but I have no suitable clothes." Which was plain unvarnished truth. "And I do not possess an opera-hat." And never did.

Kitty laughed pleasantly. "We are very democratic in this house, as by this time you will have observed. In the summer we do not dress; we take our amusements comfortably. Ordinarily we would be at our summer home on Long Island; but delayed repairs will not let us into it till August. Then we shall all take a vacation. You will join us as you are; that is, of course, if you are not too busy with your own affairs."

"Never too busy to be of service to you, Miss Killigrew. I'm only scribbling."

"A book?" — interestedly.

"Bally rot, possibly. Would you like to read it?" — one of the best inspirations he had ever had. He was not one of those silly individuals who hem and haw when some one discovers they have the itch for writing, whose sole aim is to have the secret dragged out of them, with hypocritical reluctance.

"May I?" Her friendly aloofness fell away from her as if touched by magic. "I am an inveterate reader. Besides, I know several famous editors, and perhaps I could help you."

"That would be jolly."

"And you are writing a story, and never told us about it!"

"It never occurred to me to tell you. I shall be very glad to go to the theater with you and Mrs. Killigrew."

Kitty tucked the romance under her arm and flew to her room with it. This Thomas was as full of surprises as a Christmas-box.

He eyed the empty doorway speculatively. He rather preferred the friendly aloofness; otherwise some fatal nonsense might enter his head. He resumed his chair and transferred his gaze to the blotter. He added a few pothooks by the way: numerals in addition and subtraction (for he was of Scotch descent), a name which he scratched out and scrawled again and again scratched out. He examined the contents of his wallet. How many pounds did a dress-suit cost in this hurly-burly country? This question could be answered only in one way. He hastened out into the hall, put on his hat, made for the subway, and got out directly opposite the offices of Killigrew and Company, sugar, coffee and spices. London-bred, it did not take him long to find his way about. The racket disturbed him; that was all.

The building in which Killigrew and Company had its offices belonged to Killigrew personally. It had cost him a round million to build, but the office-rentals were making it a fine investment. These ornate office-buildings caused Thomas to marvel unceasingly. In London cubby-holes were sufficient. If merchants like Killigrew, generally these were along the water-front; creaky, old, dim-windowed. In this bewildering country a man conducted his business as from a palace. The warehouses were distinct establishments.

Thomas entered the portals, stepped cautiously into one of the express-elevators (so they insisted upon calling them here), and was shot up to the fourteenth floor, all of which was occupied by Killigrew and Company. It was Thomas' first venture in this district. And he learned the amazing fact that it was ordinarily as easy to see Mr. Killigrew as it was to see King George. Office-boys, minor clerks, head clerks, managers; they quizzed and buffeted him hither and thither. He never thought to state at the outset that he was Mrs. Killigrew's private secretary; he merely said that it was very important that he should see Mr. Killigrew at once.

"Mr. Killigrew is busy," he was informed by the assistant manager, at whose desk Thomas finally arrived. "If you will give me your card I'll have it sent in to him."

Thomas confessed that he had no card. The assistant manager grew distinctly chilling.

"If you will be so kind as to inform Mr. Killigrew that Mr. Webb, Mrs. Killigrew's private secretary..."

"Why didn't you say that at once, Mr. Webb? Here, boy; tell Mr. Killigrew that Mr. Webb wishes to see him. You might just as well follow the boy."

Killigrew was smoking, and perusing the baseball edition of his favorite evening paper. All this red-tape to approach a man who wasn't doing anything more vital than that! Thomas smiled. It was a wonderful people.

"Why, hello, Webb! What's the matter? Anything wrong at the house?" — anxiously.

"No, Mr. Killigrew. I came to see you on a personal matter."

Killigrew dropped the newspaper on his desk, a little frown between his eyes. He made no inquiry.

"Miss Killigrew tells me that you will not be home this evening, and that I am to take her and Mrs. Killigrew to the theater."

"Anything in the way to prevent you?" Killigrew appeared vastly relieved for some reason.

"As a matter of fact, sir, I haven't the proper clothes; and I thought you might advise me where to go to obtain them."

Killigrew laughed until the tears started. The very heartiness of it robbed it of all rudeness. "Good lord! and I was worrying my head off. Webb, you're all right. Do you need any funds?"

"I believe I have enough." Thomas appeared to be disturbed not in the least by the older man's hilarity. It was not infectious, because he did not understand it.

"Glad you came to me. Always come to me when you're in doubt about anything. I'm no authority on clothes, but my secretary is. I'll have him take you to a tailor where you can rent a suit for to-night. He'll take your measure, and by the end of the week…" He did not finish the sentence, but pressed one of the many buttons on his desk. "Clark, this is Mr. Webb, Mrs. Killigrew's secretary. He wants some clothes. Take him along with you."

Alone again, Killigrew smiled broadly. The humor of the situation did not blind him to the salient fact that this Webb was a man of no small courage. He recognized in this courage a commendable shrewdness also: Webb wanted the right thing, honest clothes for honest dollars. A man like that would be well worth watching. And for a moment he had thought that Webb had fallen in love with Kitty and wanted to marry her! He chuckled. Clothes!

What a boy Kitty would have made! What an infallible eye she had for measuring a person! No servant-question ever dangled its hot interrogation point before his eyes. Kitty saw to that. She was the real manager of the household affairs, for all that he paid the bills. Some day she would marry a proper man; but heaven keep that day as far off as possible. What would he do without Kitty? Always ready to perch on his knee, to smooth the day-cares from his forehead, to fend off trouble, to make laughter in the house. He was not going to love the man who eventually carried her off. He was always dreading that day; young men about the house, the yacht and the summer home worried him. The whole lot of them were not worthy to tie the laces of her shoes, much as they might yearn to do so.

And all Webb wanted was a tailor! He would give a hundred for the right to tell this scare to the boys at the club, but Webb's ingenuous confidence did not merit betrayal. Still, nothing should prevent him from telling Kitty, who knew how to keep a secret. He picked up the newspaper and resumed his computation of averages (batting), chuckling audibly from time to time. Clothes!

At quarter to six Thomas returned to the house, laden with fat bundles which he hurried secretly to his room. He had never worn a dress-suit. He had often guilelessly dreamed of possessing one: between paragraphs, as another young man might have dreamed of vanquishing a rival. It was inborn that we should wish to appear well in public; to better one's condition, or, next best, to make the public believe one has. Thomas was deeply observant and quickly adaptive. Between the man who goes to school *with* books and the man who goes to school *in* books there is wide difference. What we are forced to learn seldom lifts us above the ordinary; what we learn by inclination plows our fields and reaps our harvests. It is as natural as breathing that we should like our tonics, mental as well as physical, sugar-coated.

Thomas had never worn a dress-suit; but in the matter of collars and cravats and shirts he knew the last word. But why should he wish to wear that mournfully conventional suit in which we are supposed to enjoy ourselves? She had told him not to bother about dress. Was it that very nonsense he dreaded, insidiously attacking the redoubts of his common sense?

That evening at dinner Kitty nor her mother appeared to notice the change. This gratified him; he knew that outwardly there was nothing left to desire or attain.

Kitty began to talk about the romance immediately. She had found the beginning very exciting; it was out of the usual run of stories; and if it was all as good as the first part, there would be some editors glad to get hold of it. So much for the confidence of youth. *The Black Veil*, as I have reason to know, lies at the bottom of Thomas' ancient trunk.

Long as he lived he would never forget the enjoyment of that night. The electric signs along Broadway interested him intensely; he babbled about them boyishly. Theater outside and theater within; a great drama of light and shadow, of comedy and tragedy; for he gazed upon the scene with all his poet's eyes. He enjoyed the opera, the color and music, the propinquity of Kitty. Sometimes their shoulders touched; the indefinable perfume of her hair thrilled him.

Kitty had seen all these things so many times that she no longer experienced enthusiasm; but his was so genuine, so un-English, that she found it impossible to escape the contagion. She did not bubble over, however; on the contrary, she sat through the performance strangely subdued, dimly alarmed over what she had done.

As they were leaving the lobby of the theater, a man bumped against Thomas, quite accidentally.

"I beg your pardon!" said the stranger, politely raising his hat and passing on.

"I beg your pardon!" said the stranger.

Thomas' hand went clumsily to his own hat, which he fumbled and dropped and ran after frantically across the mosaic flooring.

A ghost; yes, sir, Thomas had seen a ghost.

CHAPTER XII

I left Thomas scrambling about the mosaic lobby of the theater for his opera-hat. When he recovered it, it resembled one of those accordions upon which vaudeville artists play Mendelssohn's Wedding March and the latest ragtime (by request). Some one had stepped on it. Among the unanswerable questions stands prominently: Why do we laugh when a man loses his hat? Thomas burned with a mixture of rage and shame; shame that Kitty should witness his discomfiture and rage that, by the time he had retrieved the hat, the ghost had disappeared.

However, Thomas acted as a polished man of the world, as if eight-dollar opera-hats were mere nothings. He held it out for Kitty to inspect, smiling. Then he crushed it under his arm (where the broken spring behaved like an unlatched jack-in-the-box) and led the way to the Killigrew limousine.

"I am sorry, Mr. Webb," said Kitty, biting her lips.

"Now, now! Honestly, don't you know, I hated the thing. I knew something would happen. I never realized till this moment that it is an art all by itself to wear a high hat without feeling and looking like a silly ass."

He laughed, honestly and heartily; and Kitty laughed, and so did her mother. Subtle barriers were swept away, and all three of them became what they had not yet been, friends. It was worth many opera-hats.

"Kitty, I'm beginning to like Thomas," said her mother, later. "He was very nice about the hat. Most men would have been in a frightful temper over it."

"I'm beginning to like him, too, mother. It was cruel, but I wanted to shout with laughter as he dodged in and out of the throng. Did you notice how he smiled when he showed it to me? A woman stepped on it. When she screamed I thought there was going to be a riot."

"He's the most guileless young man I ever saw."

"He really and truly is," assented Kitty.

"I like him because he isn't afraid to climb up five flights of tenement stairs, or to shake hands with the tenants themselves. I was afraid at first."

"Afraid of what?"

"That you might have made a mistake in selecting him so casually for our secretary."

"Perhaps I have," murmured Kitty, under her breath.

Alone in her bedroom the smile left Kitty's face. A brooding frown wrinkled the smooth forehead. It was there when Celeste came in; it remained there after Celeste departed; and it vanished only under the soft, dispelling fingers of sleep.

There was a frown on Thomas' forehead, too; bitten deep. He tried to read, he tried to smoke, he tried to sleep; futilely. In the middle of the banquet, as it were, like a certain Assyrian king in Babylon, Thomas saw the Chaldaic characters on the wall: wherever he looked, written in fire — Thou fool!

CHAPTER XIII

Two mornings later the newspapers announced the important facts that Miss Kitty Killigrew had gone to Bar Harbor for the week, and that the famous uncut emeralds of the Maharajah of Something-or-other-apur had been stolen; nothing co-relative in the departure of Kitty and the green stones, coincidence only.

The Indian prince was known the world over as gem-mad. He had thousands in unset gems which he neither sold, wore, nor gave away. His various hosts and hostesses lived in mortal terror during a sojourn of his; for he carried his jewels with him always; and often, whenever the fancy seized him, he would go abruptly to his room, spread a square of cobalt-blue velvet on the floor, squat in his native fashion beside it, and empty his bags of diamonds and rubies and pearls and sapphires and emeralds and turquoises. To him they were beautiful toys. Whenever he was angry, they soothed him; whenever he was happy, they rounded out this happiness; they were his variant moods.

He played a magnificent game. Round the diamonds he would make a circle of the palest turquoises. Upon this pyramid of brilliants he would place some great ruby, sapphire, or emerald. Then his servants were commanded to raise and lower the window-curtains alternately. These shifting contra-lights put a strange life into the gems; they not only scintillated, they breathed. Or, perhaps the pyramid would be of emeralds; and he would peer into their cool green depths as he might have peered into the sea.

He kept these treasures in an ornamented iron-chest, old, battered, of simple mechanism. It had been his father's and his father's father's; it had been in the family since the days of the Peacock Throne, and most of the jewels besides. Night and day the chest was guarded. It lay upon an ancient Ispahan rug, in the center of the bedroom, which no hotel servant was permitted to enter. His five servants saw to it that all his wants were properly attended to, that no indignity to his high caste might be offered: as having his food prepared by pariah hands in the hotel kitchens, foul hands to make his bed. He was thoroughly religious; the gods of his fathers were his in all their ramifications; he wore the Brahmin thread about his neck.

He was unique among Indian princes. An Oxford graduate, he persistently and consistently clung to the elaborate costumes of his native state. And when he condescended to visit any one, it was invariably stipulated that he should be permitted to bring along his habits, his costumes and his retinue. In his suite or apartments he was the barbarian; in the drawing-room, in the ballroom, in the dining-room (where he ate nothing), he was the suave, the courteous, the educated Oriental. He drank no wines, made his own cigarettes, and never offered his hand to any one, not even to the handsome women who admired his beautiful skin and his magnificent ropes of pearls.

Some one had entered the bedroom, overpowered the guard, and looted the bag containing the emeralds. The prince, the lightest of sleepers, had slept through it all. He had awakened with a violent headache, as had four of his servants. The big Rajput who had stood watch was in the hospital, still unconscious.

All the way from San Francisco the police had been waiting for such a catastrophe. The newspapers had taken up and published broadcast the story of the prince's pastime. Naturally enough, there was not a crook in all America who was not waiting for a possible chance. Ten emeralds, weighing from six to ten carats each; a fortune, even if broken up.

Haggerty laid aside the newspaper and gravely finished his ham and eggs. "I'll take a peek int' this, Milly," he said to his wife. "We've been waiting for this t' happen. A million dollars in jools in a chest y' could open with a can-opener. Queer ginks, these Hindus. We see lots o' fakers, but this one is the real article. Mebbe a reward. All right; little ol' Haggerty can use th' money. I may not be home t' supper."

"Anything more about Mr. Crawford's valet?"

Haggerty scowled. "Not a line. I've been living in gambling joints, but no sign of him. He gambled in th' ol' days; some time 'r other he'll wander in somewhere an' try t' copper th' king. No sign of him round Crawford's ol' place. But I'll get him; it's a hunch. By-by!"

Later, the detective was conducted into the Maharajah's reception-room. The prince, in his soft drawling English (far more erudite and polished than Haggerty's, if not so direct), explained the situation, omitting no detail. He would give two thousand five hundred for the recovery of the stones.

"At what are they valued?"

"By your customs appraisers, forty thousand. To me they are priceless."

"Six t' ten carats? Why, they're worth more than that."

The prince smiled. "That was for the public."

"I'll take a look int' your bedroom," said Haggerty, rising. "Oh, no; that is not at all necessary," protested the prince.

"How d' you suppose I'm going t' find out who done it, or how it was done, then?" demanded Haggerty, bewildered.

A swift oriental gesture.

The hotel manager soothed Haggerty by explaining that the prince's caste would not permit an alien to touch anything in the bedroom while it contained the prince's belongings.

"Well, wouldn't that get your goat!" exploded Haggerty. "That lets me out. You'll have to get a clairyvoint."

The prince suggested that he be given another suite. His servants would remove his belongings. He promised that nothing else should be touched.

"How long'll it take you?"

"An hour."

"All right," assented Haggerty. "Who's got th' suite across th' hall?" he asked of the manager, as they left the prince.

"Lord Monckton. He and his valet left this morning for Bar Harbor. Back Tuesday. A house-party of Fifth Avenue people."

"Uhuh." Haggerty tugged at his mustache. "I might look around in there while I'm waiting for his Majesty t' change. Did y'ever hear th' likes? Bug-house."

"But he pays a hundred the day, Haggerty. I'll let you privately into Lord Monckton's suite. But you'll waste your time."

"Sure he left this morning?"

"I'll phone the office and make sure... Lord Monckton left shortly after midnight. His man followed early this morning. Lord Monckton went by his host's yacht. But the man followed by rail."

"What's his man look like?"

"Slim and very dark, and very quiet."

"Well, I'll take a look."

The manager was right. Haggerty had his trouble for nothing. There was no clue whatever in Lord Monckton's suite. There was no paper in the waste-baskets, in the fireplace; the blotters on the writing-desk were spotless. Some clothes were hanging in the closets, but these revealed only their fashionable maker's name. In the reception-room, on a table, a pack of cards lay spread out in an unfinished game of solitaire. All the small baggage had been taken for the journey. Truth to tell, Haggerty had not expected to find anything; he had not cared to sit idly twiddling his thumbs while the Maharajah vacated his rooms.

In the bathroom (Lord Monckton's) he found two objects which aroused his silent derision: a bottle of brilliantine and an ointment made of walnut-juice. Probably this Lord Monckton was a la-de-dah chap. Bah!

Once in the prince's vacated bedroom Haggerty went to work with classic thoroughness. Not a square foot of the room escaped his vigilant eye. The thief had not entered by the windows; he had come into the room by the door which gave to the corridor. He stood on a chair and examined the transom sill. The dust was undisturbed. He inspected the keyhole; sniffed; stood up, bent and sniffed again. It was an odor totally unknown to him. He stuffed the corner of his fresh handkerchief into the keyhole, drew it out and sniffed that. Barely perceptible. He wrapped the corner into the heart of the handkerchief, and put it back into his pocket. Some powerful narcotic had been forced into the room through the keyhole. This would account for the prince's headache. These Orientals were as bad as the Dutch; they never opened their windows for fresh air.

Beyond this faint, mysterious odor there was nothing else. The first step would be to ascertain whether this narcotic was occidental or oriental.

"Nothing doing yet," he confessed to the anxious manager. "But there ain't any cause for you t' worry. You're not responsible for jools not left in th' office."

"That isn't the idea. It's having the thing happen in this hotel. We'll add another five hundred if you succeed. Not in ten years has there been so much as a spoon missing. What do you think about it?"

"Big case. I'll be back in a little while. Don't tell th' reporters anything."

Haggerty was on his way to a near-by chemist whom he knew, when he espied Crawford in his electric, stalled in a jam at Forty-second and Broadway. He had not seen the archeologist since his return from Europe.

"Hey, Mr. Crawford!" Haggerty bawled, putting his head into the window.

"Why, Haggerty, how are you? Can I give you a lift?"

"If it won't trouble you."

"Not at all. Pretty hot weather."

"For my business. Wish I could run off t' th' seashore like you folks. Heard o' th' Maharajah's emeralds?"

"Yes. You're on that case?"

"Trying t' get on it. Looks blank jus' now. Clever bit o' work; something new. But I've got news for you, though. Your man Mason is back here again. I thought I wouldn't say nothing t' you till I put my hand on his shoulder."

"I'm sorry. I had hoped that the unfortunate devil would have had sense to remain abroad."

"Then you knew he was over there?" — quickly. "See him?"

"No. I shall never feel anything but sorry for him. You can not live with a man as I did, for ten years, and not regret his misstep."

"Oh, I understand your side. But that man was a born crook, an' th' cleverest I ever run up against. For all you know, he may have been back of a lot o' tricks Central never got hold of. I'll bet that each time that you went over with him, he took loot an' disposed of it. I may be pig-headed sometimes, but I'm dead sure o' this. Wait some day an' see. Say, take a whiff o' this an' tell me what y' think it is." Haggerty produced the handkerchief.

"I don't smell anything," said Crawford.

Haggerty seized the handkerchief and sniffed, gently, then violently. All he could smell was reminiscent of washtubs. The mysterious odor was gone.

CHAPTER XIV

This is not a story of the Maharajah's emeralds; only a knot in the landing-net of which I have already spoken. I may add with equal frankness that Haggerty, upon his own initiative, never proceeded an inch beyond the keyhole episode. It was one of his many failures; for, unlike the great fictional detectives who never fail, Haggerty was human, and did. It is only fair to add, however, that when he failed only rarely did any one else succeed. If ever criminal investigation was a man's calling, it was Haggerty's. He had infinite patience, the heart of a lion and the strength of a gorilla. Had he been highly educated, as a detective he would have been a fizzle; his mind would have been concerned with variant lofty thoughts, and the sordid would have repelled him: and all crimes are painted on a background of sordidness. In one thing Haggerty stood among his peers and topped many of them; in his long record there was not one instance of his arresting an innocent man.

So Haggerty had his failures; there are geniuses on both sides of the law; and the pariah-dog is always just a bit quicker mentally than the thoroughbred hound who hunts him; indeed, to save his hide he has to be.

Nearly every great fact is like a well-balanced kite; it has for its tail a whimsy. Haggerty, on a certain day, received twenty-five hundred dollars from the Hindu prince and five hundred more from the hotel management. The detective bore up under the strain with stoic complacency. "The Blind Madonna of the Pagan — Chance" always had her hand upon his shoulder.

Kitty went to Bar Harbor, her mother to visit friends in Orange. Thomas walked with a straight spine always; but it stiffened to think that, without knowing a solitary item about his past, they trusted him with the run of the house. The first day there was work to do; the second day, a little less; the third, nothing at all. So he moped about the great house, lonesome as a forgotten dog. He wrote a sonnet on being lonesome, tore it up and flung the scraps into the waste-basket. Once, he seated himself at the piano and picked out with clumsy forefinger *Walking Down the Old Kent Road.* Kitty could play. Often in the mornings, while at his desk, he had heard her; and oddly enough, he seemed to sense her moods by what she played. (That's the poet.) When she played Chopin or Chaminade she went about gaily all the day; when she played Beethoven, Grieg or Bach, Thomas felt the presence of shadows.

There was a magnificent library, mostly editions de luxe. Thomas smiled over the many uncut volumes. True, Dickens, Dumas and Stevenson were tolerably well-thumbed; but the host of thinkers and poets and dramatists and theologians, in their hand-tooled Levant...! Away in an obscure corner (because of its cheap binding) he came across a set of Lamb. He took out a volume at random and glanced at the fly-leaf — "Kitty Killigrew, Smith College." Then he went into the body of the book. It was copiously marked and annotated. There was something so intimate in the touch of the book that he felt he was committing a sacrilege, looking as it were into

Kitty's soul. Most men would have gone through the set. Thomas put the book away. Thou fool, indeed! What a hash he had made of his affairs!

He saw Killigrew at breakfast only. The merchant preferred his club in the absence of his family.

Early in the afternoon of the fourth day, Thomas received a telephone call from Killigrew.

"Hello! That you, Webb?"

"Yes. Who is it?"

"Killigrew. Got anything to do to-night?"

"No, Mr. Killigrew."

"You know where my club is, don't you?"

"Yes."

"Well, be there at seven for dinner. Tell the butler and the housekeeper. Mr. Crawford has a box to the fight to-night, and he thought perhaps you'd like to go along with us."

"A boxing-match?"

"Ten rounds, light-weights; and fast boys, too. Both Irish."

"Really, I shall be glad to go."

"Webb?"

"Yes."

"Never use that word 'really' to me. It's un-Irish."

Thomas heard a chuckle before the receiver at

the other end clicked on the hook. What a father this hearty, kindly, humorous Irishman would have made for a son!

In London Thomas' amusements had been divided into three classes. During the season he went to the opera twice, to the music-halls once a month, to a boxing-match whenever he could spare the shillings. He belonged to a workingmen's club not far from where he lived; an empty warehouse, converted into a hall, with a platform in the center, from which the fervid (and often misinformed) socialists harangued; and in one corner was a fair gymnasium. Every fortnight, for the sum of a crown a head, three or four amateur bouts were arranged. Thomas rarely missed these exhibitions; he seriously considered it a part of his self-acquired education. What Englishman lives who does not? Brains and brawn make a man (or a country) invincible.

At seven promptly Thomas called at the club and asked for Mr. Killigrew. He was shown into the grill, where he was pleasantly greeted by his host and Crawford and introduced to a young man about his own age, a Mr. Forbes. Thomas, dressed in his new stag-coat, felt that he was getting along famously. He had some doubt in regard to his straw hat, however, till, after dinner, he saw that his companions were wearing their Panamas.

Forbes, the artist, had reached that blasé period when, only upon rare occasions, did he feel disposed to enlarge his acquaintance. But this fresh-skinned young Britisher went to his heart at once, a kindred soul, and he adopted him forthwith. He and Thomas paired off and talked "fight" all the way to the box-ing club.

There was a great crowd pressing about the entrance. There were eddies of turbulent spirits. A crowd in America is unlike any other. It is full of meanness, rowdyism, petty malice. A big fellow, smelling of bad whisky, shouldered Killigrew aside, roughly. Killigrew's Irish blood flamed.

"Here! Look where you're going!" he cried.

The man reached back and jammed Killigrew's hat down over his eyes. Killigrew stumbled and fell, and Crawford and Forbes surged to his rescue from the trampling feet. Thomas, however, caught the ruffian's right wrist, jammed it scientifically against the man's chest, took him by the throat and bore him back, savagely and relentlessly. The crowd, packed as it was, gave ground. With an oath the man struck. Thomas struck back, accurately. Instantly the circle widened. A fight outside was always more interesting than one inside the ropes. A blow ripped open Thomas' shirt. It became a slam-bang affair. Thomas knocked his man down just as a burly policeman arrived. Naturally, he caught hold of Thomas and called for assistance. The wrong man first is the invariable rule of the New York police.

"Milligan!" shouted Killigrew, as he sighted one of the club's promoters.

Milligan recognized his millionaire patron and pushed to his side.

After due explanations, Thomas was liberated and the real culprit was forced swearing through the press toward the patrol-wagon, always near on such nights. Eventually the four gained Crawford's box. Aside from a cut lip and a torn shirt, Thomas was uninjured. If his fairy-godmother had prearranged this fisticuff, she could not have done anything better so far as Killigrew was concerned.

"Thomas," he said, as the main bout was being staged, the chairs and water-pails and paraphernalia changed to fresh corners, "I'll remember that turn. If you're not Irish, it's no fault of yours. I wish you knew something about coffee."

"I enjoy drinking it," Thomas replied, smiling humorously.

Ever after the merchant-prince treated Thomas like a son; the kind of a boy he had always wanted and could not have. And only once again did he doubt; and he longed to throttle the man who brought into light what appeared to be the most damnable evidence of Thomas' perfidy.

CHAPTER XV

We chaps who write have magic carpets.

Whiz!

A marble balcony, overlooking the sea, which shimmered under the light of the summer moon. Lord Henry Monckton and Kitty leaned over the baluster and silently watched the rush of the rollers landward and the slink of them back to the sea.

For three days Kitty had wondered whether she liked or disliked Lord Monckton. The fact that he was the man who had bumped into Thomas that night at the theater may have had something to do with her doddering. He might at least have helped Thomas in recovering his hat. Dark, full-bearded, slender, with hands like a woman's, quiet of manner yet affable, he was the most picturesque person at the cottage. But there was always something smoldering in those sleepy eyes of his that suggested to Kitty a mockery. It was not that recognizable mockery of all those visiting Englishmen who held themselves complacently superior to their generous American hosts. It was as though he were silently laughing at all he saw, at all which happened about him, as if he stood in the midst of some huge joke which he alone was capable of understanding: so Kitty weighed him.

He did not seem to care particularly for women; he never hovered about them, offering little favors and courtesies; rather, he let them come to him. Nor did he care for dancing. But he was always ready to make up a table at bridge; and a shrewd capable player he was, too.

The music in the ballroom stopped.

"Will you be so good, Miss Killigrew, as to tell me why you Americans call a palace like this — a cottage?" Lord Monckton's voice was pleasing, with only a slight accent.

"I'm sure I do not know. If it were mine, I'd call it a villa."

"Quite properly."

"Do you like Americans?"

"I have no preference for any people. I prefer individuals. I had much rather talk to an enlightened Chinaman than to an unenlightened white man."

"I am afraid you are what they call blasé."

"Perhaps I am not quite at ease yet. I was buffeted about a deal in the old days."

Lord Monckton dropped back into the wicker chair, in the deep shadow. Kitty did not move. She wondered what Thomas was doing. (Thomas was rubbing ointment on his raw knuckles.)

"I am very fond of the sea," remarked Lord Monckton. "I have seen some odd parts of it. Every man has his Odyssey, his Aeneid."

Aeneid. It seemed to Kitty that her body had turned that instant into marble as cold as that under her palms.

The coal of the man's cigar glowed intermittently. She could see nothing else.

Aeneid — Enid.

CHAPTER XVI

Thomas slammed the ball with a force which carried it far over the wire backstop.

"You must not drive them so hard, Mr. Webb; at least, not up. Drive them down. Try it again."

Tennis looked so easy from the sidelines that Thomas believed all he had to do was to hit the ball whenever he saw it within reach; but after a few experiments he accepted the fact that every game required a certain talent, quite as distinct as that needed to sell green neckties (old stock) when the prevailing fashion was polka-dot blue. How he loathed Thomas Webb. How he loathed the impulse which had catapulted him into this mad whirligig! Why had not fate left him in peace; if not satisfied with his lot, at least resigned? And now must come this confrontation, the inevitable! No poor rat in a trap could have felt more harassed. Mentally, he went round and round in circles, but he could find no exit. There is no file to saw the bars of circumstance.

That the lithe young figure on the other side of the net, here, there, backward and forward, alert, accurate, bubbling with energy... Once, a mad rollicking impulse seized and urged him to vault the net and take her in his arms and hold her still for a moment. But he knew. She was using him as an athlete uses a trainer before a real contest.

There was something more behind his stroke than mere awkwardness. It was downright savagery. Generally when a man is in anger or despair he longs to smash things; and these inoffensive tennis-balls were to Thomas a gift of the gods. Each time one sailed away over the backstop, it was like the pop of a safety-valve; it averted an explosion.

"That will be enough!" cried Kitty, as the last of a dozen balls sailed toward the distant stables.

The tennis-courts were sunken and round them ran a parapet of lawn, crisp and green, with marble benches opposite the posts, generally used as judges' stands. Upon one of these Kitty sat down and began to fan herself. Thomas walked over and sat down beside her. The slight gesture of her hand had been a command.

It was early morning, before breakfast; still and warm and breathless, a forerunner of a long hot summer day. A few hundred yards to the south lay the sea, shimmering as it sprawled lazily upon the tawny sands.

The propinquity of a pretty girl and a lonely young man has founded more than one story.

"You'll be enjoying the game, once you learn it."

"Do you think I ever will?" asked Thomas. He bent forward and began tapping the clay with his racket. How to run away!

Kitty, as she looked down at his head, knew that there were a dozen absurd wishes in her heart, none of which could possibly ever become facts. He was so different from the self-assertive young men she knew, with their silly flirtations, their inane small-talk, their capacity for Scotch whisky and long hours. For days she had studied him as through microscopic lenses; his guilelessness was real. It just simply could not be; her ears had deceived her that memorable foggy night in London. And yet, always in the dark his voice was that of one of the two men who had talked near her cab. Who was he? Not a single corner of the veil had he yet lifted, and here it was, the middle of August; and except for the week at Bar Harbor she had been with him day by day, laid she knew not how many traps, over which he had stepped serenely, warily or unconsciously she could not tell which. It made her heart ache; for, manly and simple as he appeared, honest as he seemed, he was either a rogue or the dupe of one, which was almost as bad. But to-day she was determined to learn which he was.

"What have you done with the romance?"

"I have put it away in the bottom of my trunk. The seventh rejection convinces me that I am not a story-teller."

He had a desperate longing to tell her all, then and there. It was too late. He would be arrested as a smuggler, turned out of the house as an impostor.

"Don't give up so easily. There are still ninety-three other editors waiting to read it."

"I have my doubts. Still, it was a pleasant pastime." He sat back and stared at the sea. He must go this day; he must invent some way of leaving. Then came the Machiavellian way; only, he managed as usual to execute it in his blundering English style. Without warning he dropped his racket, caught

Kitty in his arms tightly and roughly, kissed her cheek, rose, and strode swiftly across the courts, into the villa. It was done. He could go now; he knew very well he had to go.

His subsequent actions were methodical enough; a shower, a thorough rub-down, and then into his workaday clothes. He packed his trunk and hand-luggage, overlooked nothing that was his, and went down into the living-room where he knew he would find Killigrew with the morning papers. He felt oddly light-headed; but he had no time to analyze the cause.

"Good morning, Thomas," greeted the master of the house cordially.

"I am leaving, Mr. Killigrew. Will you be kind enough to let me have the use of the motor to the station?"

"Leaving! What's happened? What's the matter? Young man, what the devil's this about?"

"I am sorry, sir, but I have insulted Miss Killigrew."

"Insulted Kitty?" Killigrew sprang up.

"Just a moment, sir," warned Thomas. The tense, short but powerful figure of Kitty's father was not at that moment an agreeable thing to look at; and Thomas knew that those knotted hands were rising toward his throat. "Do not misinterpret me, sir. I took Miss Kitty in my arms and kissed her."

"You — kissed — Kitty?" Killigrew fell back into his chair, limp. For a moment there had been black murder in his heart; now he wondered whether to weep or laugh. The reaction was too sudden to admit of coherent thought. "You kissed Kitty?" he repeated mechanically.

"Yes, sir."

"What did she do?"

"I did not wait to learn, sir."

Killigrew got up and walked the length of the room several times, his chin in his collar, his hands clasped behind his back, under his coat-tails. The fifth passage carried him out on to the veranda. He kept on going and disappeared among the lilac hedges.

Thomas thought he understood this action, that his inference was perfectly logical; Killigrew, rather than strike the man who had so gratuitously insulted his daughter, had preferred to run away. (I know; for a long time I, too, believed Thomas the most colossal ass since Dobson.) Thomas gazed mournfully about the room. It was all over. He had burned his bridges. It had been so pleasant, so homelike; and he had begun to love these unpretentious people as if they had been his very own.

Except that which had been expended on clothes, Thomas had most of his salary. It would carry him along till he found something else to do. To get away, immediately, was the main idea; he had found a door to the trap. (The chamois-bag lay in his trunk, forgotten.)

"Your breakfast is ready, sir," announced the

grave butler.

So Thomas ate his chops and potatoes and toast and drank his tea, alone.

And Killigrew, blinking tears, leaned against the stout branches of the lilacs and buried his teeth in his coat-sleeve. He was as near apoplexy as he was ever to come.

CHAPTER XVII

Meantime Kitty sat on the bench, stunned. Never before in all her life had such a thing happened. True, young men had at times attempted to kiss her, but not in this fashion. A rough embrace, a kiss on her cheek, and he had gone. Not a word, not a sign of apology. She could not have been more astounded had a thunder-bolt struck at her feet, nor more bereft of action. She must have sat there fully ten minutes without movement. From Thomas, the guileless, this! What did it mean? She could not understand. Had he instantly begged forgiveness, had he made protestations of sentiment, a glimmering would have been hers. Nothing; he had kissed her and walked away: as he might have kissed Celeste, and had, for all she knew!

When the numbing sense of astonishment passed away, it left her cold with anger. Kitty was a dignified young lady, and she would not tolerate such an affront from any man alive. It was more than an affront; it was a dire catastrophe. What should she do now? What would become of all her wonderfully maneuvered plans?

She went directly to her room and flung herself upon the bed, bewildered and unhappy. And there Killigrew found her. He was a wise old man, deeply versed in humanity, having passed his way up through all sorts and conditions of it to his present peaceful state.

"Kittibudget, what the deuce is all this about?... You've been crying!"

"Supposing I have?" — came muffled from the pillows.

"What have you been doing to Thomas?"

"I?" she shot back, sitting up, her eyes blazing. "He kissed me, dad, as he probably kisses his English barmaids."

"Kitty, girl, you're as pretty as a primrose. I don't think Thomas was really accountable."

"Are you defending him?" — blankly.

"No. The strange part of it is, I don't think Thomas wants to be defended. A few minutes ago he came to me and told me what he had done. He is leaving."

The anger went out of her eyes, snuffed — candle-wise. "Leaving?"

"Leaving. He asked me for the motor to the station."

"Leaving! Well, that's about the only possible thing he could do, under the circumstances. He has a good excuse." Excuse! Kitty's nimble mind reached out and touched Thomas' Machiavellian inspiration.

"Hang it, Kitty, I had to run out into the lilacs to laugh! Can't this be smoothed over some way? I like that boy; I don't care if he is a Britisher and sometimes as simple as a fool. When I think of the other light-headed duffers who call themselves gentlemen ... Pah! They drink my whiskies, smoke my cigars, and dub me an old Mick behind my back. They run around with silly chorus-girls and play poker till sun-up, and never do an honest day's work. It takes a brave man to come to me and frankly say that he has insulted my daughter."

"He said that?" Behind her lips Kitty was already smiling. "You are acting very strangely, dad."

"I know. Ordinarily I'd have taken him by the collar and hustled him into the road. And if it had been one of those young bachelors who are coming down to-night, I'd have done it. I like Thomas; and I don't think he kissed you either to affront or to insult you."

"Indeed!" — icily.

"I dare say I stole a kiss or two in my day."

"Does mother know it?"

"Back in the old country, when I was a lad. It's a normal impulse. There isn't a young man alive who can look upon a pretty girl's face without wishing to kiss it. I don't believe Thomas will repeat the offense. The trouble, girl, is this — you've been living in a false atmosphere, where people hide all their generous impulses because to be natural is not fashionable."

"I marvel at you more and more. Is it generous, then, to kiss a girl without so much as by your leave? If he had been sorry, if he had apologized, I might overlook the deed. But he kissed me and walked away. Do you realize what such an action means to any young woman with pride? Very well, if he apologizes he may stay; but no longer on the basis of friendship. It must be purely business. When my

117

guests arrive I shall not consider it necessary to ask him to join any of our amusements."

"Poor devil! He'll have to pay for that kiss."

"Next, I suppose you'll be wanting me to marry him!" Kitty volleyed. But she wasn't half so angry as she pretended.

"What? Thomas?"

"Ah, that's different, isn't it? There, there; I've promised to overlook the offense on condition that he apologize and keep his place. I have always said that you'd rather have a man about than me."

"Well, perhaps I could understand a man better."

"Go down to breakfast. I hear mother moving about. I'll ring for what I need. I must bathe and dress. Some of the people will motor in for lunch."

Killigrew, subdued and mystified, went in search of Thomas and discovered him in almost the exact spot he had left him; for Thomas, having breakfasted, had returned to the living-room to await the motor.

"Thomas, when Kitty comes down, apologize. And remember this, that you can't kiss a pretty girl just because you happen to want to."

"But, Mr. Killigrew, I didn't want to!" said Thomas.

"Well, I'll be tinker-dammed!"

"I mean... Really, sir, it is better that I should return at once to the city. I'm a rotter."

"Don't be a fool! Take your grips back to your room, and don't let's have any more nonsense. Finish up that report from Brazil; and if you handle it right, I'll take you into the office where you'll be away from the women folks."

Thomas' heart went down in despair.

"Mrs. Killigrew can find another secretary for the bureau. I shan't say a word to her, and I'll see that Kitty doesn't. You've had your breakfast. Go and finish up that report. Williams," Killigrew called to the second man, "take Mr. Webb's grips up to his rooms. I'll see you later, Thomas," and Killigrew made off for the breakfast-room, where he chuckled at odd times, much to his wife's curiosity. But he shook his head when she quizzed him.

"You agree with me, Molly, don't you, that Kitty shall marry when and where she pleases?"

"Certainly, Daniel. I don't believe in ready-made matches."

"No more do I. Molly, old girl, I've slathers of money. I could quit now; but I'm healthy and can't play all day. Got to work some of the time. Every one around here shall do as they please. And," — slyly — "if Kitty should want to marry Thomas..."

"Thomas?"

"Anything against the idea?"

"But Thomas couldn't take care of Kitty."

"H'm."

"And Kitty wouldn't marry a man who couldn't."

"Some truth In that. At present Thomas couldn't support an idea. But there's makings in the boy, give a man time and nothing else to do. There's one thing, though; Thomas seems to have the gift of picking out the chaff when it comes to men. A man who can spot a man is worth something to somebody. Where Thomas' niche is, however, I can't tell to date. He'll never get on socially; he has too much regard for other people's feelings."

"And no tact."

"A poor man needs a good deal of that." Killigrew began paring his fourth chop-bone. He hadn't enjoyed himself so much in months. Thomas had kissed Kitty and hadn't wanted to!

It would take a philosopher to dig up the reason for that; or rather a clairvoyant, since philosophers dealt only with logical sequences, and there was nothing logical to Killigrew's mind in Thomas kissing Kitty when he hadn't wanted to!

CHAPTER XVIII

Sugar, coffee and spices. Thomas dipped his pen into the inkwell and went to work. Were all American fathers mad? To condone an affront like this! He could not understand these Americans. He had approached Killigrew with far more courage than the latter suspected. Thomas had read that here men still shot each other on slight provocation. Sugar, coffee and spices... Sao Paulo and valorization committee... 10,000,000 bags. What should he do? Whither should he turn? To have offered that affront... for nothing! Kitty, whom he revered above all women save one, his mother!... Sugar, coffee and spices. Rio number seven, 7 1/2 to 13 1/2 cents. Leaks in the roasting business... Apologize? On his knees, if need be. Caught like a rat in a trap; done for; at the end of his rope. Why hadn't he taken to his heels when he had had the chance? Gone at once to New York and sent for his belongings?... Sugar, coffee and spices... The pen slipped from his fingers, and he laid his head on his arms. Monumental ass!

Up suddenly, alert eyed. There was a telephone-booth in the hall. This he sought noiselessly. He remained hidden in the booth for as long as twenty minutes. Then he emerged, wiping the perspiration from his forehead. For the time being he was saved. But he was very miserable.

Sugar, coffee and spices again. Doggedly he recommenced the transcription, adding, deducting, comparing. He heard a slight noise by the portière, and raised his eyes. Kitty stood there like a picture in a frame; pale, calm of eye.

He was on his feet quickly. "Miss Killigrew, I apologize for my unwarranted rudeness. I did not mean it as you thought I did" — which would have made any other woman furious.

"I know it," said Kitty to herself. "You wanted an excuse to run away. All my conjectures are true. I believe I have you, Mr. Thomas, right in the hollow of my hand." To Thomas, however, she was a presentiment of cold and silent indignation.

He blundered on. "You have all been so kind to me... I am sorry. I am also quite ready to stay or go, whichever you say."

"We shall say no more about it," she replied coldly; turned on her trim little heels and went out into the rose gardens, where she found fault with the head gardener; and on to the stables, where she rated the head groom for not exercising her favorite mount; and back to the villa, where she upset the cook by ordering a hearty breakfast which she could not eat; and all the time striving to smother her generous impulses and the queer little thrills which stirred in her heart.

Guests began to arrive a little before luncheon. A handsome yacht joined Killigrew's in the offing. Laughter and music began to be heard about the villa.

Thomas took his documents and retired to his room, hoping they would forget all about him. He had luncheon there. About four o'clock he looked out of the window toward the beach. They were in bathing; half a dozen young men and women. The diving-raft bobbed up and down. Only yesterday she had tried to teach him how to swim. After all, he was only a bally haberdasher's clerk; he would never be anything more than that.

More guests for dinner, which Thomas also had in his room, despite Killigrew's protests. The villa would be filled for a whole week, and a merry dance he would have to avoid the guests. At nine, just as he was on the point of going to bed, the second man knocked for admittance.

"Miss Killigrew wishes you to come aboard the visiting yacht at ten, sir."

"Offer Miss Killigrew my excuses. I am very tired."

"Miss Killigrew was decided, sir. Her father's orders. He wishes you to meet his resident partner in Rio Janeiro. Mr. Killigrew and Mr. Savage will be in the smoke-room forward, sir."

"Very well. Tell Miss Killigrew that I shall come aboard."

"Thank you, sir. The motor-boat will be at the jetty at nine-thirty, sir." The servants about the Killigrew home understood Thomas' position. They had known young honorables who had served as private secretaries.

A formal command. There was no way of avoiding it. Resignedly Thomas got into his evening clothes. They might smile at his pumps, the hang of his coat, but there would be no question over the correctness of his collar and cravat. He was very bitter against the world, and more especially against Thomas Webb, late of Hodman, Pelt and Company, "haberdashers to H. H. the Duke of" and so forth and so on.

All the way down to the motor-boat his new pumps sang "Fool-fool! Rotter-rotter!" He climbed the yacht's ladder and ran into Kitty and her guests, exactly as she had arranged he should.

"Mr. Webb," she said; and immediately began introducing him, leaving Lord Henry Monckton until the last. A cluster of lights made the spot as bright as day.

Thomas bowed politely and Lord Monckton smiled amiably.

"Mr. Killigrew is in the smoking-room?" Thomas inquired.

"Yes."

Thomas bowed again, indirectly toward the guests and walked away. Lord Monckton commented on the beauty of the night.

And Kitty caught the gasp between her teeth, lest it should be heard. Fog!

CHAPTER XIX

"Rather hot for this time of day," volunteered Lord Monckton, sliding into the Morris chair at the side of Thomas' desk and dangling his legs over the arm.

"Yes, it is," agreed Thomas, folding a sheet of paper and placing the little ivory elephant paper-weight upon it.

"Rippin' doubles this morning. You ought to go into the game. Do you a lot of good."

"I didn't know you played."

"Don't. Watch."

Thomas' gaze was level and steady.

Lord Monckton laughed easily and sought his monocle. He fumbled about the front of his coat and shirt. "By jove! Lost my glass; wonder I can see any-thing."

Outside, on the veranda, the two men could see the cluster of women of which Kitty was the most animated flower. Voices carried easily.

"Ah — what do you think of these — ah — Americans?" asked Lord Monckton, as one compa-triot to another, leaning toward the desk.

"I think them very kindly, very generous peo-ple; at least, those I have met. Have you not found them so?"

"Quite so. I am enjoying myself immensely." Lord Monckton swung about in the chair, his back to the veranda.

Thomas loosened his negligee linen-collar.

"Ah, really!" drifted into the room. Lord Monckton sleepily eying Thomas, only heard the voice; he did not see, as Thomas did, the action and gesture which accompanied the phrase. Kitty had put something into her eye, squinted, and twisted an imaginary something a few inches below her dimpled chin. It was a hoydenish trick, but Kitty had enacted it for Lord Monckton's benefit. The women shouted with laughter. Lord Monckton turned in time to see them troop into the gardens. He turned again to Thomas, to find a grin upon that gentleman's face.

It was a hoydenish trick

It was a hoydenish trick.

"Miss Killigrew is rather an unusual young person," was his comment.

"Uncommon," replied Thomas, scrutinizing the point of his pen.

"For my part, I prefer 'em clinging." Lord Monckton rose.

"Rotter!" breathed Thomas. He rearranged his papers, crackling them suggestively.

"Picnic this afternoon; going along?" asked Lord Monckton, pausing by the portières.

"Really, I am not a guest here; I am only private secretary to Mrs. Killigrew. If they treat me as a human being it is because they believe that charity should not play in grooves."

"Ah! We are all open to a little charity."

"That's true enough. Good morning."

"Beggar!" murmured Lord Monckton as he let the portières fall behind him.

"Blighter!" muttered Thomas, staring malevolently at the empty doorway. He would be glad when Mr. and Mrs. Crawford and the artist came down. Forbes was a chap you could get along with anywhere, under any conditions.

Some time later Kitty came in. She crossed immediately to the desk. As Thomas looked up, she smiled at him. It was the first smile of the kind he had witnessed, coming in his direction, since before that blunder on the tennis-courts.

"I found Lord Monckton's monocle, Mr. Webb. Will you be so kind as to give it to him?"

"Yes, Miss Killigrew." Absently he raised the monocle and squinted through it. "Why, it's plain glass!" he exclaimed.

"So it is," replied Kitty, with a crooked smile. "And I dare say so are most of the monocles we see. A silly affectation, don't you think so?"

He was instantly up in arms. The monocle was a British institution, and he would as soon have denied the divine right of kings as question an Englishman's right to wear what he pleased in his eye.

"It was originally designed for a man whose left eye was weaker than the right. Besides, we don't notice them over there."

"I have often wondered what the wearers do when their noses itch."

"Doubtless they scratch them."

Kitty's laughter bubbled. It subsided instantly. Her hand reached out, then dropped. She had almost said: "Thomas, what have you done with my sapphires?" Urgent as the impulse was, she crushed it back. For deep in her heart she wanted to believe in Thomas; wanted to believe that it was only a mad wager such as Englishmen propose, accept and see to the end. There was not the slightest doubt in her mind that Thomas and Lord Monckton were the two men who had stood on the curb that foggy night in London. One had taken the necklace and the other had wagered he would carry it six months in America before returning it to its owner. The Nana Sahib's ruby she attributed to a real thief, who had known Crawford in former days and, conscience-stricken, had returned it.

Great Britain was an empire of wagerers she knew; they wagered for and against every conceivable thing which had its dependence on chance.

That first night on board the Celtic, when Thomas came to her cabin in the dark, she had recognized his voice. In the light the activity of the eye had dulled the keenness of the ear; but in the dark the ear had found the chord. For days she had been subconsciously waiting to hear one or the other of those voices; and Thomas' had come with a shock. The words "Aeneid" and "Enid" had so little variation in sound between them that Kitty had found her second man in Lord Monckton. Sooner or later she would trap them.

"Would you like to go to the picnic this afternoon?" — with a spirit which was wholly kind.

"Very much indeed; but I can't" — indicating the stack of papers on his desk.

"Oh," listlessly.

"I am very poor, Miss Killigrew, and perhaps I am ambitious."

Her lips parted expectantly.

"Your father has promised to give me a chance on his coffee plantations in Brazil this autumn, and I wish to show him that I know how to grind. Plug, isn't that the American for it?" He smiled across the desk. "I wish to prove to you all that I am grateful. Your father, who knows something of men, says there is one hidden away in me somewhere, if only I'll take the trouble to dig it out. I should like to be with you and your guests all the time. I like play, and I have been very lonely all my life." He fingered the papers irresolutely. "My place is here, not with your guests; there's the width of the poles between us. I ought not to know anything about the pleasures of idleness till the day comes when I can afford to."

"Perhaps you are right," she admitted. What an agreeable voice he had! Perhaps neither of them was a rogue; only a wild pair of Englishmen embarked on a dangerous frolic. "Don't forget to give Lord Monckton his monocle."

"I shan't."

Kitty departed, smiling. Her thought was: he had kissed her and hadn't wanted to! (Ah, but he had; and not till long hours after did he realize that there had been as much Thomas as Machiavelli in that futile inspiration!)

Report 47, on the difference between the shipments to Europe and America. Very dry, very dull; what with the glorious sunshine outside and the chance to play, Report 47 was damnable. A bird-like peck at the inkwell, and the pen began to scratch-scratch-scratch. He was twenty-four; by the time he was thirty he ought to…

"Beg pardon, sir!"

Lord Monckton's valet stood before the desk. Thomas did not like this man, with his soundless approaches, his thin nervous fingers, his brilliant roving eyes. Where had he been picked up? A perfect servant, yes; but it seemed to Thomas that the man was always expecting some one to come up behind him. Those quick cat-like glances over his shoulder were not reassuring. Dark, swarthy; and yet that odd white scar in the scalp above his ear. That ought to have been dark, logically.

"What is it?"

"Lord Monckton has dropped his glass somewhere, sir, and he sent me to inquire, sir."

"Oh, here it is. And tell your master to be very careful of it. Some one might step on it."

"Thank you, sir." The valet departed as noiselessly as he had entered.

"Really," mused Thomas, "there's a rum chap. I don't like him around. He gives me the what-d'-y'-call-it."

They needed an extra man at the table that night, so Thomas came down. He found himself between two jolly young women, opposite Kitty who divided her time between Lord Monckton and a young millionaire who, rumor bruited it, was very attentive to Killigrew's daughter. Still, Thomas enjoyed himself. Nobody seemed to mind that he was only a clerk in the house. The simpleton did not realize that he was a personage to these people; an English private secretary, quite a social stroke on the part of the Killigrews.

He gathered odd bits of news of what was going on among the summer colonists. The lady next to Killigrew, a Mrs. Wilberforce, had had a strange adventure the night before. She and her maid had been mysteriously overpowered by some strange fume, and later discovered that her pearls were gone. She had notified the town police. This brought the conversation around to the maharajah's emeralds. Hadn't he and his attendants been overcome in the same manner? Thomas thought of the sapphires. Since nobody knew he had them, he stood in no danger. But there was Kitty's great fire-opal, glowing like a coal on her breast, seeming to breathe as she breathed. It was almost as large as a crown-piece.

During lulls Thomas dreamed. He was going to give himself until thirty to make his fortune; and he was going to make it down there in the wilds of South America. But invariably the sleepy mocking eyes of Lord Monckton brought him back to earth, jarringly.

Once, Kitty caught Thomas gazing malevolently at Lord Monckton. No love lost between them, evidently. It was the ancient story: to wager, to borrow, to lend, to lose a friend.

Long after midnight Kitty awoke. She awoke hungry. So she put on her slippers and peignoir and stole down-stairs. The grills on each side of the entrance to the main hall were open; that is, the casement windows were thrown back. She heard voices and naturally paused to learn whose they were. She would have known them anywhere in the world.

"Tut, tut, Tommy; don't be a bally ass and lose your temper."

"Temper? Lose my temper? I'm not losing it, but I'm jolly well tired of this rotten business."

"It was you who suggested the wager; I only accepted it."

"I know it."

"And once booked, no Englishman will welch, if he isn't a cad."

"I'm not thinking of welching. But I don't see what you get out of it."

"Sport. And a good hand at bridge."

"Remarkably good."

"I say, you don't mean to insinuate…"

"I'm not insinuating. I'm just damnably tired. Why the devil did you take up that monocle business? You never wore one; and Miss Killigrew found out this morning that it was an ordinary glass."

"She did?" Lord Monckton chuckled.

"And she laughed over it, too."

"Keen of her. But, what the devil! Stick a monocle in your eye, and you don't need any letters of introduction. Lucky idea, your telephoning me that you were here. What a frolic, all around!"

So that was why her coup had fallen flat? thought Kitty.

"I'll tell you this much," said Thomas. (Kitty heard him tap his pipe against the veranda railing.) "Play fair or, by the lord, I'll smash you! I'm going to stick to my end of the bargain, and see that you walk straight with yours."

"I see what's worrying you. Clear your mind. I would not marry the richest, handsomest woman in all the world, Thomas. There's a dead heart inside of me."

"There's another thing. I'd get rid of that valet."

"Why?" — quickly.

"He's too bally soft on his feet to my liking. I don't like him."

"Neither do I, Thomas!" murmured Kitty, forgetting all about her hunger. Not a word about her sapphires, though. Did she see but the surface of things? Was there something deeper?

She stole back up-stairs. As she reached the upper landing, some one brushed past her, swiftly, noiselessly. With the rush of air which followed the prowler's wake came a peculiar sickish odor. She waited for a while. But there was no sound in all the great house.

CHAPTER XX

"The Carew cottage was entered last night," said Killigrew, "and twenty thousand in diamonds are gone. Getting uncomfortably close. You and your mother, Kitty, had better let me take your jewels into town to-day."

"We have nothing out here but trinkets."

"Trinkets! Do you call that fire-opal a trinket? Better let me take it into town, anyway. I'm Irish enough to be superstitious about opals."

"That's nonsense."

"Maybe."

"Oh, well; if the thought of having it around makes you nervous, I'll give it to you. The Crawfords and Mr. Forbes are coming down this afternoon. You must be home again before dinner. Here's the opal." She took it from around her neck.

"Crawfords? Fine!" Killigrew slipped the gem into his wallet. "I'll bring them back on the yacht if you'll take the trouble to phone them to meet me at the club pier."

"I'll do so at once. Good-by! Mind the street-crossing," she added, mimicking her mother's voice.

"I'll be careful," he laughed, stepping into the launch which immediately swung away toward the beautiful yacht, dazzling white in the early morning sunshine.

Kitty waved her handkerchief, turned and

walked slowly back to the villa. Who had passed her in the upper hall? And on what errand? Neither Thomas nor Lord Monckton, for she had left them on the veranda. Perhaps she was worrying unnecessarily. It might have been one of her guests, going down to the library for a book to read.

She met Lord Monckton coming out.

"Fine morning!" he greeted. He made a gesture, palm upward.

A slight shiver touched the nape of Kitty's neck. She had never noticed before how frightfully scarred his thumbs and finger-tips were. He saw the glance.

"Ah! You notice my fingers? Not at all sensitive about them, really. Hunting a few years ago and clumsily fell on the camp-stove. Scar on my shoulder where I struck as I rolled off. Stupid. Tripped over a case of canned corn. I have fingers now as sensitive as a blind man's."

"I am sorry," she said perfunctorily. "You must tell me of your adventures."

"Had a raft of 'em. Mr. Killigrew gone to New York?"

"For a part of the day. Had your breakfast?"

"No. Nothing to do; thought I'd wait for the rest of them. Read a little. Swim this morning, just about dawn. Refreshing."

"Then I'll see you at breakfast."

He smiled and stepped aside for her to pass. She proved rather a puzzle to him.

Kitty spent several minutes in the telephone booth.

She began to realize that the solution of the Webb-Monckton wager was as far away as ever. Lord Monckton was leaving on the morrow. She must play her cards quickly or throw them away. The fact that neither had in any way referred to the character of the wager left her in a haze. Sometime during the day or evening she must maneuver to get them together and tell them frankly that she knew everything. She wanted her sapphires; more, she wanted the incubus removed from Thomas' shoulders. Mad as March hares, both of them; for they had not the least idea that the sapphires were hers!

Later, she stole to the library door and peered in. Thomas was at his desk. For a long time she watched him. He appeared restless, uneasy. He nibbled the penholder, rumpled his hair, picked up the ivory elephant and balanced it, plunged furiously into work again, paused, stared at the Persian carpet, turned the inkwell around, worked, paused, sighed. Thomas was very unhappy. This state of mind was quite evident to Kitty. Kissed her and hadn't wanted to. He was unlike any young man she knew.

Presently he began to scribble aimlessly on the blotter. All at once he flung down the pen, rose and walked out through the casement-doors, down toward the sea. Kitty's curiosity was irresistible. She ran over to the blotter.

Fool!

Blighter!

Rotter!

Double-dyed ass!

Blockhead!

Kitty Killigrew — (scratched out)!

Nincompoop!

Haberdasher!

Ass!

All of which indicated to the investigator that Thomas for the present had not a high opinion of himself. An ordinary young woman would have laughed herself into hysterics. Kitty tore off the scribbles, not the least sign of laughter in her eyes, and sought the window-seat in the living-room. There was one word which stood out strangely alien: haberdasher. Why that word? Was it a corner of the curtain she had been striving to look behind? Had Thomas been a haberdasher prior to his steward-ship? And was he ashamed of the fact?

Haberdasher.

What's the matter with that word? If it irked Thomas it irked Kitty no less. It is a part of youth to crave for high-sounding names and occupations. It is in the mother's milk they feed on. Mothers dream of their babes growing up into presidents or at least ambassadors, if sons; titles and brilliant literary sa-lons, if daughters. What living mother would harbor a dream of a clerkship in a haberdasher's shop? Per-ish the thought! Myself for years was told that I had as good a chance as anybody of being president of the United States; a far better chance than many, being as I was *my* mother's son.

Irish blood and romance will always be mysteriously intertwined. Haberdasher did not fit in anywhere with Kitty's projects; it was off-key, a jarring note. Whoever heard of a haberdasher's clerk reading *Morte d'Arthur* and writing sonnets? She was reasonably certain that while Thomas had jotted it down in scornful self-flagellation, it occupied a place somewhere in his past.

"They turne out ther trashe And shew ther haberdashe, Ther pylde pedlarye."

There's no romance in collars and cuffs and ties and suspenders.

CHAPTER XXI

Meanwhile Killigrew arrived in New York, went to the bank and deposited Kitty's opal, and sought his office.

"There's a Mr. Haggerty in your office, Mr. Killigrew. I told him to wait."

"Haggerty, the detective?"

"Yes. He said you'd be glad to see him. Has news of some sort."

Killigrew hurried into his private office. "Hello, Haggerty! What's the trouble this morning?"

"Got some news for you." Haggerty accepted a cigar. "I've a hunch that I can find Miss Killigrew's sapphires."

"No! I thought they had been sold over the other side."

"Seems not."

"Got your man?"

"Nope. Funny kind of a job, though. Fooled th' customs inspectors. Sapphires 'r here in New York, somewheres."

"A thousand to you, Haggerty, if you recover them."

"A row between two stewards on th' *Celtic* gave me th' clue."

"Why, that's the boat I came over on."

"Sure thing."

"And the thief was on board all the time?"

"Don't think he was when you crossed. I've got t' wait till th' boat docks before I can get particulars. It's like this. Th' chap who took th' sapphires engaged passage as a steward. His cabin-mate saw him lookin' over th' stones. He'd taken 'em out o' their settings. This man Jameson pinches 'em, but his mate follows him up an' has it out with him in a waterfront groggery. Got 'em back. Cool customer. I went on board th' next morning an' quizzed him. An' say, he done me up brown. As unblinkin' a liar 's I ever met. Took me t' his cabin an' showed me what he professed Jameson had swiped. Nothing but a pearl an' coral brooch. He did it so natural that I swallowed th' bull, horns an' hoofs. I've had every pawnshop in New York looked over, but they ain't there. I've been busy on the maharajah's emeralds. There's a case. Cleverest ever. Some drug, atomized through a keyhole, which puts y' t' by-by."

"A drug? Why, say, two of my neighbors have been robbed within the past three days, and they all complained of violent headaches."

"Well, what y' know about that! Say, Mr. Killigrew, any place where I could hang out down there for a couple o' days?"

"Come as my guest, Haggerty. I can tell the folks that you're from the office."

"Fumes! I'll bet a hat it's my maharajah's man. When do you go back?"

"About half-past two, on my yacht. You'll find it at the New York Yacht Club pier. Some old friends of yours will be on board. Crawford, his wife, and Forbes, the artist."

"Fine an' dandy! Forbes is clever at guessing, an' we'll work t'gether. All right I'll hike up t' Bronx an' get some duds. Tell th' chef that corn-beef an' cabbage is my speed-limit," jested the detective as he reached the door.

"By the way, what's the name of that steward who took my daughter's sapphires?"

"His monacker is Webb," said Haggerty; "Thomas Webb, Esquire; an' believe me, he's some smooth guy. Thomas Webb."

CHAPTER XXII

For a moment Killigrew sat stiffly upright in his chair; then gradually his body grew limp, his chin sank, his shoulders drooped. "Webb?" he said dully. "Are you sure, Haggerty?"

"No question about it. Y' see, this Jameson chap writes me a sassy letter from Liverpool. Spite. Thomas Webb was th' name. What's th' matter?"

"Haggerty, the very devil is the matter. Thomas Webb, recently a steward on the *Celtic*, has been my wife's private secretary for nearly two months."

"Say that again!" gasped Haggerty, bracing himself against the jamb of the door.

"But I'll wager my right hand that there's some mistake."

"Of all th' gall I ever heard of! Private secretary, an' Miss Killigrew's sapphires stowed away in his trunk, if he ain't sold 'em outside th' pawnshops! Will y' gimme a free hand, Mr. Killigrew?"

"I suppose I'll have to."

"All right. On board you draw me a map o' th' rooms an' where Thomas Webb holds out. I shan't come t' th' house an' meet anybody. While you folks 'r at supper I'll sneak up t' his room an' see what's in his trunk. If I don't find 'em, why, I'll come back t' town an' start a news stand, Forty-second an' Broadway. I'll be on th' yacht at half-past two. I'm on m' way."

The door behind him closed with a bang. It startled every clerk on the huge floor. The door to the boss' office did not bang more than once a year, and that was immediately after the annual meeting of the directors of the Combined Brazilian Coffees. Who was this potentate who dared desecrate the honored quiet of this loft?

Haggerty's news hit Killigrew hard. Thomas. There must be a mistake. He had not studied men all these years without learning to read young and old with creditable accuracy. Thomas was as easy to read as an amateur's scorecard; runs were runs, hits were hits, outs were outs. Why, Thomas wouldn't have stolen an apple from a farmer's orchard — without permission. What, enter a carriage in a fog, steal a necklace, and carry it around with him for months? Never in this world. And private secretary to the very person he had robbed? Of all the fool situations, this was the cap! Imbecility was written all over the face of it. It was simply a coincidence in the matter of names. Yet, steward on the *Celtic*; there was no getting away from that. There could not have been two Thomas Webbs on board. I'm afraid Killigrew swore; distant thunder, off behind the hills there. He struck the desk with his balled fist. He knew it; it was that infernal opal of Kitty's getting in its deadly work. And what would Kitty say? What would she do?

He stood up and pulled down the roller-top violently. The crash of it sent every clerk, book-keeper and stenographer huddling over his or her work. Two bangs all in one morning? What had happened to the coffee market? As a matter of fact, coffee fell off a quarter point between then and closing; which goes to prove that the stock-market depends upon its business less in the matter of supply and demand than in "signs."

On board the yacht Killigrew laid the affair before Crawford.

"What do you believe?"

"I've reached the point," said Crawford, "where I believe in nothing except this young lady," and he laid his hand over his wife's. "For ten years I had a valet named Mason. I would have staked my life on his integrity, his honesty. He turned out to be an accomplished rogue. Went with me into the wilds of Africa and Persia, through deserts, swamps, over mountains; tireless, resourceful, dependable; and saved my life twice. Its knocked a hole in my faith in mankind."

"Listen here," said Haggerty. "Without your knowing it, he always carried a bunch o' first-class skeleton keys. I'm dead sure he was working his game all th' time. He came back for them keys, but he didn't get 'em. He's in New York somewheres. D' y' think y' could recognize him if y' saw him?"

"Instantly."

"A man can change his looks in two years," said Forbes. "Remember File Number 113?"

"This is real life, Mort; not a detective story."

"How would you recognise him?"

"That I'm unable to explain. It's what Haggerty here calls a hunch."

Haggerty nodded. "An' if y' depend on 'em y' generally land. I've made some mistakes in my time, not believing in my hunches. This Webb business goes t' show. I had a hunch that something was wrong, but your Webb had such a kid face, th' hunch pulled for him. Well, if y' ever see Mason again, what'll y' do?"

"I don't know. It's a tough proposition. Somehow or other, I want to be quits with Mason. I want to wipe out those obligations. If I could do that, the next time I saw him I'd hand him over."

"You're a sentimental duffer, Crawffy," said the artist, smiling.

"And I shouldn't love him at all if he wasn't," the wife defended.

"But this Webb affair doesn't add up right," said Killigrew morosely.

"There's th' hull game," declared Haggerty. "It's nothing but adding an' subtracting, this gum-shoe work. Y've got t' keep at it till it adds right. Y' don't realize, Mr. Crawford, how many times I almost put my hand on your shoulder; but y' didn't add up right. I shan't go at Webb like a load o' bricks. I'll nose around first. Take a peek int' his belongings while you folks keep him busy downstairs. No sapphires, no Thomas; I'll let it go at that. But how was this man Jameson t' know anything about sapphires if they wasn't any?"

"I've known Kitty Killigrew ever since she was born," said Killigrew dryly. "I've yet to see her make a mistake in sizing up a man. She picks 'em out the way I do, right off the bat. The minute you dodder about a man or a woman, there's sure to be something' to dodder about. Good lord! you don't suppose he had a hand in these other burglaries?"

"Can't say 's I do," answered Haggerty, reaching for his lemonade. "You wait. I'll have it all cleared up by midnight, 'r they'll be a shake-up at Central t'-morrow. Something's going t' happen; feel it like a sailor feels a storm when they ain't a cloud anywheres. Now, let's see what y' know about auction pinochle, Mr. Killigrew. No use moping."

The yacht dropped anchor off shore at five. The beach was deserted. Doubtless the guests were cat-napping or reading. At the Killigrew villa one did as one pleased. Mr. and Mrs. Crawford were shown to their rooms at once, and Haggerty prowled about the stables and garage. Kitty knocked at Mrs. Crawford's door half an hour later.

Introductions were made at dinner. The Crawfords knew most of Kitty's guests and so did Forbes, who was very much interested in Lord Monckton. Here was a romance, if there was any truth at all in the newspapers. What adventures here and there across the world before the title fell to him! He looked like one of R. Caton Woodville's drawings of Indian mutiny officers, with that flowing black beard; very conspicuous among all these smooth chins. Forbes determined to sketch him.

He was rather sorry not to see Thomas at the table. Was Haggerty after him with the third degree? Poor devil! It did not seem possible; yet all the evidence pointed to Thomas. Why should Jameson say that he had seen sapphires if he had not? Still, the thing that did not add up was the position with which Thomas had allied himself to the Killigrews. Hang it, there was a figure missing. Haggerty was right. A man with any sympathy had no business man-hunting.

After dinner Crawford sought Forbes. "Have you any fire-arms with you, Mort?" he whispered.

"A pair of automatics. Why…"

"Sh! Please hustle and get them and ask no questions. Hurry!"

CHAPTER XXIII

"Mr. Killigrew," whispered Haggerty, "will you get Miss Kitty an' Thomas int' th' study-end o' th' library?"

"Found anything?"

"Th' sapphires were in his trunk, all right. Tucked away in th' toes of a pair o' shoes. Webb is in th' library now. Jus' get Miss Kitty."

"Very well," replied Killigrew, leaden-hearted.

Thomas had been busy all day. He was growing very tired, and often now the point of his pen sputtered. The second man had brought in his dinner and set it on a small stand which stood at the right of the desk. It was growing cold on the tray. A sound. He glanced up wearily. He saw Kitty and Killigrew, and behind them the sardonic visage of Haggerty. Thomas got up slowly.

"Take it easy, Mr. Webb," warned Haggerty. "Go on, Miss Killigrew, an' we'll see first if you've hit it."

Thomas stared, wide-eyed, from face to face. What in heaven's name had happened? What was this blighter of a detective doing at the villa? And why was Kitty so white?

"Mr. Webb," began Kitty, striving hard to maintain even tones, "on the night of May 13, you and Lord Henry Monckton stood on the curb outside my carriage, near the Garden, where I was blockaded in the fog. I heard your voices. There was talk about a wager. The time imposed upon the fulfilment of this wager was six months. Shortly after, Lord Monckton entered my carriage under the pretense of getting into his own and took my necklace of sapphires. He did it very cleverly. Then they were turned over to you. You were to carry them for six months, find out to whom they belonged, and return them."

"Thousands of miles away," said Haggerty confidently. "Nothing ever happened like that."

"Is it not true?" asked Kitty, ignoring Haggerty's interpolation.

"Miss Killigrew, either I'm dreaming or you are. I haven't the slightest idea what you are talking about." Thomas was now whiter than Kitty. "The talk about a wager is true; but I never knew you had lost any sapphires."

"How about this little chamois-bag which I found in your trunk, Mr. Webb?" asked Haggerty ironically. He tossed the bag on the desk.

The bag hypnotized Thomas. Suddenly he came to life. He snatched up the bag and thrust it into his pocket.

"Those are mine," he said quite calmly. "Mine, by every legal and moral right in the world. Mine!"

Kitty breathed hard and closed her eyes.

"Some brass!" jeered Haggerty, stepping forward.

"Can you prove it, Thomas?" asked Killigrew, hoping against hope.

"Yes, Mr. Killigrew, to your satisfaction, to Miss Killigrew's, and even to Mr. Haggerty's."

Tableau.

Broken by the entrance of Crawford and Forbes, who were also pale and disturbed. Crawford flung a packet of papers on the desk.

"Webb, I fancy that these papers are yours," said Crawford, smiling.

One glance was enough for Thomas.

"Tell them the truth," went on Crawford; "tell them who you are."

"I have wagered…"

"Never mind about the wager," put in Forbes. "Crawford and I have just canceled it."

"What has happened?" asked Thomas. The whole world seemed tumbling about his unhappy head.

"Tell Mr. Killigrew here how you have imposed on him and his family," urged Crawford, serious now. "Tell them your name, your full name."

Thomas hesitated a moment. "My name is Henry Thomas Webb-Monckton."

"Ninth Baron of Dimbledon," added Forbes, "and as crazy as a loon!"

CHAPTER XXIV

Meanwhile the whirligig had gone about violently after this fashion.

Forbes, wondering mightily, procured his automatics and gave one to his impatient friend.

"What's the row, Crawffy?"

"Be as silent as you can," said Crawford. "Follow me. We may be too late."

"Anywhere you say."

"The door will be locked. We'll creep around the upper veranda and enter by opposite windows. You keep your eye on the valet. Don't be afraid to shoot if it's necessary."

"What the deuce…!"

"Come!"

"But where?"

"Lord Monckton's room."

Blindly and confidently Forbes went out the rear window of the corridor, while Crawford made for the front. They crept soundlessly forward. Lord Monckton? What was up? Shoot the valet if necessary! All right; Crawford knew what he was doing. He generally did. Through his window Forbes saw two men packing suit-cases furiously. The moment Crawford entered the room, Forbes did likewise, without the least idea what it was all about.

"Put up your hands!" said Crawford quietly.

Master and man came about face.

"H'm! The dyed beard and stained skin might fool any one but me, Mason."

Mason! Forbes' hand shook violently.

"I have seen you with a beard before, in the days when we hadn't time for razors. I knew you the instant I laid eyes on you. Now, then, a few words. I do not care to stand in your debt. Haggerty is downstairs. Upon two occasions you saved my life… Keep your eye on your man, Forbes!… Twice you saved my life. I'm going to give you a chance in return. An hour's start, perhaps. Forbes, come over to me. That's it. Give me the automatic. There. Now, go through their pockets carefully, and put everything in your own. Leave the money. Mason, a boat leaves tomorrow noon for Liverpool. I'll ship your trunks and grips to the American Express Company there. Do you understand? If I ever see you again, I shan't lift a finger to save you."

The late Lord Henry Monckton shrugged. He had not lived intimately with this quiet-voiced man for ten years without having acquired the knowledge that he never wasted words.

"You're a dangerously clever man, Mason. I noted at dinner that in some manner you had destroyed Haggerty's photograph of your finger-tips. But I recognize you, and know you — your gestures, the turn of your head, every little mannerism. And if you do not do as I bid, I'll take my oath in court as to your identity. Besides," — with a nod toward the suitcases — "if you're not the man, why this hurry?

An hour. I see, fortunately, you have already changed your clothes. Be off!"

"All right. I'm Mason. I knew the game was up the moment I saw you. Any one but you, Mr. Crawford, would pay for this interruption, pistol or no pistol. An hour. So be it. You might tell that fool down-stairs and give him the papers you find in my grip. Miss Killigrew's sapphires, I regret to say, are no more. The mistake I made in London was in returning the Nana Sahib's ruby."

"There is always one mistake," replied Crawford sternly. He felt sad, too.

"Off with you, Tibbets! We can make the train for New York if we hustle."

The man-servant's brilliant eyes flashed evilly.

"Will you make it an hour and a half, sir?" asked Mason, as his valet slid over the window-sill.

It sounded strange to Forbes. Mason had unconsciously fallen into the old tone and mode of address, and he himself recognized him now.

"Till nine-thirty, then. At that time I shall notify Haggerty."

"The boat?"

"Oh, no. I'm giving you that chance without conditions. It's up to Haggerty to find you. There's one question I should like to ask you. Were you in this sort of business while you were serving me?"

Mason laughed. The real man shone in his eyes and smile. "I was. It was very exciting. It was very amusing, too. I valeted you during the day-time and went about my own peculiar business at night. I entered your service to rob you and remained to serve you; ten years. I want you always to remember this: to you I was loyal, that I stood between you and death because you were the only being I was fond of. You are the one bit of sentiment that ever entered my life. Well, I must be off. But I've had a jolly time of it, masquerading as a titled gentleman. What a comedy! How the fools kotowed and simpered while I looked over their jewels and speculated upon how much I could get for them! But I had my code. I never pilfered in the houses of my hosts. I set a fine trap for that simple young man down-stairs, and he fell into it, head-first. Trust an Englishman of his sort to see nothing beyond his nose. I'm off. Good-by, Mr. Crawford. I'm grateful." The man stepped out of the window and vanished into the night.

Crawford glanced at his watch; it was eight-ten.

"Do you hope he'll get away?" asked Forbes breathlessly.

"I don't know what I hope, Mort. I'm rather dazed with the unexpectedness of all this. Let's see what you took from their pockets."

A large diamond brooch, a string of fine pearls, and a bag of wonderful polished emeralds.

"Mort, the man couldn't help it. Why, here's a fortune for a prince; and yet he remained here for more. Well, he's gone; poor beggar."

They burrowed into the suit-cases and trunks. A dark green bottle came to light, Forbes took out the cork and carelessly sniffed. A great black wave of dizziness swept over him, and he would have fallen but for Crawford. The bottle fell. Crawford put Forbes out into the hall and ran back for the bottle, sensing a slight dizziness himself. He recognized the odor. It was Persian. He and Mason had run across it unpleasantly, once upon a time, in Teheran. He was not familiar with the chemistry of the concoction. He corked the bottle tightly. Forbes came in groggily.

"Well! Did you ever see such an ass, Crawford? To open a strange bottle like that and sniff at it!"

"Here's an atomizer. They must have used that. Never touched their victims."

"It evaporates quickly, though. But the effect on a sleeping person would be long. Now, who the deuce is this chap Webb? A confederate?"

"Still dizzy, eh? No; Thomas is a dupe. Don't you get it? He's Lord Monckton. Come on; we'll go down and straighten out the kinks."

So they went down-stairs. And Forbes tells me that when Thomas acknowledged his identity, Kitty did not fall on his neck. Instead, she walked up to him, burning with fury: so pretty that Forbes almost fell in love with her, then and there.

"So! You pretended to be poor, and entered my home to make play behind our backs! Despicable! We took you in without question, generously, kindly, and treated you as one of us; and all the while you were laughing in your sleeve!"

"Kitty!" remonstrated Killigrew, who felt twenty

years gone from his shoulders.

"Let me be! I wish him to know exactly what I think of his conduct." She whirled upon the luckless erstwhile haberdasher's clerk; but he held out his hand for silence. He was angry, too.

"Miss Killigrew, I entered your employ honestly. I was poor. I am poor. I have had to work for my bread every day of my life. For seven years I was a clerk in a haberdasher's shop in London. And one day the solicitors came and notified me that I had fallen into the title, two hundred and twenty pounds, and those sapphires. The estate was so small and so heavily mortgaged that I knew I could not live on it. The rents merely paid the interest. I was no better off than before. The cash was all that was saved out of an annuity." From his inner waist-coat pocket he produced a document and dropped it on the desk. "There is the solicitor's statement, relative to the whole transaction. And now I'll tell you the rest of it. I've been a fool. I was always more or less alone. I met this man Cavenaugh, or whatever he calls himself, in a concert-hall about a year ago. We became friendly. He came to me and bought his collars and ties and suspenders."

Kitty found herself retreating from a fury which far outmatched her own; and as he gained in force, hers dwindled correspondingly.

Thomas continued. "He was well-read, traveled; he interested me. When the title came, he was first to congratulate me. Gave me my first real dinner. Naturally I was grateful for this attention. Well, the upshot of it was, we gambled; and I lost. There was wine. I suggested in the spirit of madness that I play the use of my title for six months against the money I had lost. He agreed. And here I am."

His fury evaporated. He sank back into his chair and rested his head in his hands.

"I ain't a detective," murmured Haggerty, breaking in on the silence which ensued. "I'm only fit t' chase dagos selling bananas without licenses. But I'm aching t' see this other chap. I kinda see through his game. He's going t' interest me a hull lot." Crawford consulted his watch again. Nine. "Haggerty, suppose you and I knock the billiard balls around for half an hour?"

"Huh?"

"Half an hour."

"I got t' see that chap, Mr. Crawford."

"It's a matter of four or five thousand. Do you want to risk it?"

"Come on, Haggerty!" cried Forbes, with good understanding. He caught the detective by the arm and pulled him toward the door. But Haggerty hung back sturdily.

"Is this straight, Mr. Crawford?"

"Half an hour; otherwise not a penny."

"All well an' good; but I'll hold you responsible if anything goes wrong. I'm not seeing things clear."

"You will presently."

"Four thousand for half an hour?"

"To a penny."

"You're on!"

The three of them marched off to the billiard-room. Killigrew touched Kitty's arm and motioned her to follow. She was rather glad to go. She was on the verge of most undignified tears. When she had gone in search of Mrs. Crawford, Killigrew walked over to Thomas and laid a hand on the young man's shoulder.

"Thomas, will you go to Brazil the first week in September?"

"God knows, I'll be glad to," said Thomas, lifting his head. His young face was colorless and haggard. "But you are putting your trust in a double-dyed ass."

"I'll take a chance at that. Now, Thomas, as no doubt you're aware, we are all Irish in this family. Hot-tempered, quick to take affront, but also quick to forgive or admit a wrong. You leave Kitty alone till to-morrow."

"I believe it best for me to leave to-night, sir."

"Nothing of the sort. Come out into the cooler, and we'll have a peg. It won't hurt either of us, after all this racket."

*****

Half after nine. Crawford laid down his cue. From his pocket he took a bottle and gravely handed it to Haggerty.

159

"Smell of the cork, carefully," Crawford advised.

Haggerty did so. "Th' stuff they put th' maharajah t' sleep with!"

Then Forbes emptied his pockets.

"Th' emeralds!" shouted Haggerty.

Suddenly he stiffened. "I'm wise. I know. It's your man Mason, an' you've bunked me int' letting him have all this time for his get-away!"

CHAPTER XXV

"That is true, Haggerty. I had a debt to pay." Crawford spun a billiard ball down the table.

"Mr. Crawford, I'm going t' show you that I'm a good sport. You've challenged me. All right. I want that man, an' by th' Lord Harry, I'm going t' get him. I'm going t' put my hand on his shoulder an' say 'Come along!' Cash ain't everything, even in my business. I want t' show it's th' game, too. I don't want money in my pockets for winking my eye."

"You'll have hard work."

"How?"

"He has burned the pads of his fingers and thumbs," blurted out Forbes.

Crawford made an angry gesture.

A Homeric laugh from Haggerty. "I don't want his fingers now; this bottle an' these emeralds are enough for me." He stuffed the jewels away. "Where's th' phone?"

"In the hall, under the stairs."

"Good night."

The nights of Poe and the grim realities of Balzac would not serve to describe that chase. The magnificent vitality of that man Haggerty yet fills me with wonder. He borrowed a roadster from Killigrew's garage, and hummed away toward New York. On the way he laid his plans of battle, winnowed the chaff from the grain. He understood the necessity of thinking and acting quickly. A sporting proposition, that was it. He wanted just then not so much the criminal as the joy of finding him against odds and laying his hand on his shoulder: just to show them all that he wasn't a has-been.

His telephone message had thrown a cordon of argus-eyed men around New York. Now, then, what would he, Haggerty, do if he were in Mason's shoes? Make for railroads or boats; for Mason did not belong to New York's underworld, and he would therefore find no haven in the city. Boat or train, then; and of the two, the boat would offer the better security. Once on board, Mason would find it easy to lose his identity, despite the wireless. And it all hung by a hair: would Mason watch? If he hid himself and stayed hidden he was saved.

"Chauffeur, what's your name?" asked Haggerty of Killigrew's man, as the car rolled quietly on to Brooklyn Bridge.

"Harrigan," — promptly.

"That's good enough for me," — jovially. "Fill up th' gas-tank. I'm going t' keep y' busy for twenty-four hours, mebbe. An' if I win, a hundred for yours. All y' got t' do is t' act as I say. Let 'er go. Th' Great White Way first, where th' hotels hang out."

Lord Monckton had not returned to the hotel. Good. More telephoning. Yes, the great railroad terminals had ten men each. A black-bearded man with scarred fingers.

Haggerty was really a fine general; he directed his army with shrewdness and little or no waste. The

Jersey side was watched, East and North Rivers. The big ships Haggerty himself undertook.

From half after nine that night till noon the next day, without sleep or rest or food, excepting a cup of coffee and a sandwich, which, to a man of Haggerty's build, wasn't food at all, he searched. Each time he left the motor-car, the chauffeur fell asleep. Haggerty reasoned in this wise: There were really but two points of departure for a man in Mason's position, London or South America. Ten men, vigilant and keen-eyed, were watching all fruiters and tramps which sailed for the Caribbean.

It came to the last boat. Haggerty, in each case, had not gone aboard by way of the passengers' gangplank; not he. He got aboard secretly and worked his way up from hold to boat-deck. His chance lay in Mason's curiosity. It would be almost impossible for the man not to watch for his ancient enemy.

At two minutes to twelve, as the whistle boomed its warning to visitors to go ashore, Haggerty put his hard-palmed hand on Mason's shoulder. The man, intent on watching the gangplank, turned quickly, sagged, and fell back against the rail.

"Come along," said Haggerty, not unkindly.

Mason sighed. "One question. Did Mr. Crawford advise you where to look for me?"

"No. I found you myself, Mr. Mason; all alone. It was a sporting proposition; an' you'd have won out if y' hadn't been human like everybody else, an' watched for me. Come along!"

CHAPTER XXVI

It remains for me, then, to relate how Thomas escaped that arm of the law equally as relentless as that of the police — the customs. Perfectly innocent of intent, he was none the less a smuggler.

Killigrew took him before the Collector of the Port, laid the matter before him frankly, paid the duty, and took the gems over to Tiffany's expert, who informed him that these sapphires were the originals from which his daughter's had been copied, and were far more valuable. Twenty-five thousand would not purchase such a string of sapphires these days. All like a nice, calm fairy-story for children.

Immediately upon being informed of his wealth, Thomas became filled with a truly magnanimous idea. But of that, later.

A week later, to be exact.

Around and upon the terrace of the Killigrew villa, with its cool white marble and fresh green strip of lawn, illumined at each end by scarlet poppy-beds, lay the bright beauty of the morning. The sea below was still, the air between, and the heavens above, since no cloud moved up or down the misty blue horizons. Leaning over the baluster was a young woman. She too was still; and her eyes, directed toward the sea, contemplative apparently but introspective in truth, divided in their deeps the blue of the heavens and the green of the sea. Presently a sound broke the hush. It came from a neat little brown shoe. Tap-tap, tap-tap. To the observer of infinite details, a foot is often more expressive than lips or eyes. Moods must find some outlet. One can nearly perfectly control the face and hands; the foot is least guarded.

The young man by the nearest poppy-bed plucked a great scarlet flower. Luckily for him the head gardener was not about. Then slowly he walked over to the young woman. The little foot became still.

"I am sailing day after to-morrow for Rio Janeiro," he said. He laid on the broad marble top of the baluster a little chamois-bag. "Will you have these reset and wear them for me?"

"The sapphires? Why, you mustn't let them go out of the family. They are wonderful heirlooms."

"I do not intend to let them go out of the family," he replied quietly.

Kitty stirred the bag with her fingers. She did not raise her eyes from it. In fact, she would have found it difficult to look elsewhere just then.

"Will you wear them?"

"Yes."

"And some day will you call me Thomas?"

"Yes... When you return."

Somewhere back I spoke of Magic Carpets we writer chaps have. A thing of flimsy dreams and fancies! But I forgot the millionaire's. His is real, made of legal-tenders woven intricately, wonderfully. Does he wish a palace, a yacht, a rare jewel? Whiz! There you are, sir. No flowery flourishes; the cold, hard, beautiful facts of reality. Killigrew had his Magic Carpet, and he spread it out and stood on it as he and Mrs. Killigrew viewed the pair out on the terrace. (The millionaire can sometimes wish happiness with his Carpet.)

"Molly, I'm going to send Thomas down to Rio. He'll be worth exactly fifteen hundred the year... for years. But I'm going to give him five thousand the first year, ten thousand the next, and twenty thereafter... if he sticks. And I think he will. He'll never be any the wiser." He paused tantalizingly.

"Well?" demanded Mrs. Killigrew, smiling.

"Well, neither will Kitty."